THE DIAMOND MURDER

An addictive crime mystery full of twists

(Eric Ward Book 4)

ROY LEWIS

JOFFE BOOKS

Revised edition 2019
Joffe Books, London

First published as "Once Dead, Twice Dying", 1984

ISBN 978-1-78931-183-9

CHAPTER 1

It was two in the morning before they came.

There were three of them, standing huddled together in the morning cold of the woods, a dark, silent group. The undergrowth matched their silence: it was as though the woods were waiting for something to happen and the silence seemed to affect the three dogs, making them crouch down in the tense darkness, quivering, eager. One of the men lit a cigarette, the red glow bringing a momentary metallic gleam from the spade carried by the man beside him. The third man shuffled uneasily. When he spoke, it was in a low, impatient mutter.

'Where the 'ell is he, man?'

'Said he'd be here. He'll come, will Jack.'

The minutes lengthened, and the figures of the waiting men merged into the dark shadows of the tall trees on the hill. A light breeze rose, soughing coldly through the undergrowth, and the cigarette described a glowing arc through the air, flicked away by an impatient finger. 'Howway, you hear that?'

The low rumbling sound came from the far end of the field below the copse, in the direction of Rothbury Crags. The regular beat of the engine was broken on the night air, caught up in the breeze, but as it grew closer, and louder, it was recognizable as the engine of a tractor, and a few moments later the first glow of its headlights touched the fringe of the copse, harshening the lines of the trees. The three men and the dogs moved forward, towards the distant glow, and they stood at the bottom of the slope, awaiting the tractor as it came rumbling towards them across the field.

Above them, on their knees in the undergrowth, the two watchers crouched low, the one clutching his flash apparatus with numb fingers, the other craning forward to watch the approach of the tractor. It seemed as though they were going to be lucky, after all.

The tractor crossed the field, trundled through the shallow water of the burn, and lurched into the slope of the hill as it headed for the copse. It rumbled forward, the roar of its engine echoing in the silence and the man with the spade, raising his hand, was caught briefly in the headlights, whitening through the trees and casting fantastic, elongated shadows across the slope.

The dogs were up now, whimpering, excited as the night air was broken by the laborious progress of the tractor, churning forward to the edge of the treeline, coming to a halt at the bottom of the slope and then manoeuvring patiently until its harsh headlights beamed through the trees on the steep side of the hill.

The driver stood up behind his wheel, black against the reflected glare of the headlights. 'Awright, Frank?'

'Great, man, great! Thass fine, Jack: now we can see what we're bloody well doin'!'

The tractor-driver cut his engine; the end of the noise made the silence seem loud to the watchers on the hill. The driver, Jack, scrambled down from his seat and made his way through the pool of light and into the trees, towards the spot where the three men waited. Something glinted in his left hand: a long piece of steel. He used it to thrust into the earth, an aid to the climb up the slope, but the watchers knew that it would serve a different purpose in a little while.

One of the dogs yelped a welcome as the tractor-driver joined the others; someone opened a flask and as the men below stood in a tight little group, talking in low voices among themselves, the faint odour of coffee drifted up the hill.

A few minutes later the group began to break up, the men fanning out a little, checking the ground within the range of the tractor headlights, with the dogs prancing, whimpering in subdued excitement, until one of them, the man called Frank, raised his hand. He had found what they were looking for.

The four of them stood in a tight circle on the steep wooded slope, while the dogs thrust inquisitive noses between their legs and the man called Jack drove the long steel probe into the soft earth, where the tunnels had been dug that year. One of the dogs, black in the light of the tractor headlights, was pushing forward eagerly, but was kicked back with a muffled curse; the others stood stifflegged, quivering with anticipation as the steel probe went in, again and again.

The group broke up in a sudden flurry of excitement. Two men seized dogs; the man called Frank grabbed the black dog and dragged it forward, thrusting it into the hole in the ground so that it disappeared with an excited wriggling. There was a short silence, but the air was electric with expectancy, and once again, as a deep thumping noise came from the tunnel, there was a flurry of activity. A second dog was dragged forward, thrust down into the tunnel behind the first and the steel probe was cast aside. The tractor-driver moved forward; in his hand he carried an instrument that began to buzz loudly, like a geiger counter.

'Bring the shovel!'

The tractor-driver stood to one side as one of the men started to dig. The buzzing continued, a harsh, abrasive sound that was punctuated by the gasping of the man with the shovel as he dug swiftly in the soft earth. Within minutes he was succeeded by one of the others, thrust aside impatiently as he slowed, so that the furious digging lost no impetus, each man taking his turn in brief spasms of wild activity, and in the bright light of the tractor headlights the watchers on the hill could see, as the black earth was thrown aside, that the men had broken into the tunnel.

The thumping noise from below the ground was continuing, and now there was also another sound, a muffled yapping and barking that was punctuated by savage growling sounds. Suddenly the surge of activity with the shovel ceased, it was thrown aside, and in the tunnel the grey and white flanks of a large badger could be seen.

Pandemonium broke loose. 'Work 'im, work 'im!' one of the men was shouting and the two remaining dogs threw themselves forward in a furious whirl of snapping and barking. The men again started to dig furiously and the bumping noise grew louder as the animal's flanks heaved madly in the tunnel. In the demonic light of the tractor's headlamps it was all suddenly clear as the big sow badger emerged, the terrier's teeth sunk into the fur near the animal's throat, and the watchers knew that the bumping noise had come from dog and badger tugging and wrestling with each other in the sett.

The other two dogs had settled their teeth into the badger's fur and there was a shout of triumph as one of the hunters leaned forward, grabbed the thirty-five-pound badger by its tail and dragged it from its tunnel, swinging it high with the straining dogs still hanging on to it. In the harsh light they could all see its bloodstained sides as it hung, struggling, writhing and twisting its head in an attempt to bite its tormentor. The men were shouting and laughing, almost drunk with excitement, and one of the dogs fell off, barking, only to leap in and snap at the struggling badger again.

It was at that moment that Eddie Stevens said '*Now!*' to the photographer, and the man stood up, unnoticed by the hunters below, paused, then took three quick photographs in succession.

The brightness of the flash was almost blinding in spite of the light from the tractor. One of the men yowled in his surprise, the burly man holding the badger swore violently and then with one great swing of his arm sent the animal hurtling twenty feet away down the hill. The dogs set up an excited yammering as the badger crashed into the undergrowth, picked itself up and ran off in a trail of blood. The four men in the glow of the tractor's headlights paid no attention. They stared up the slope to where the two men stood.

'What the 'ell do you think you're doin'?'

Eddie Stevens said quietly to the photographer, 'Pack your gear, don't rush, just do it quietly.'

'I said, what the bloody 'ell you up to?' The burly man who had held up the badger began to move forward, menacingly. 'Who are you?'

'We're reporters from the *Star*,' Eddie Stevens said. 'What you've been doing is illegal and we—'

'Hey, you just wait there!' The burly man shouted and quickened his step, plunging forward into the hill.

'Bloody hell!' the photographer said, and then, humping his gear, turned and stumbled off through the trees. Eddie Stevens hesitated for a moment, uncertain, but as the other three men below began to hurry after their leader he too turned, and began to run. Their car was at the other side of the copse; they'd been told that if they parked there and made their way through the copse they might remain unseen while the badger-hunters indulged in their sport, but it meant now that there was some distance to run in the darkness through the trees if they were to get back to the safety of the car.

He heard the photographer swearing and cursing off to his left and he himself made as much noise as he could, swinging right, aware that if the hunters caught the photographer they would certainly destroy his gear and his film. It would be a nice little scoop for the *Star*, a shot of the badger-hunters caught in the act, and with luck he might even be able to sell it to one of the Sundays. But not if the hunters got hold of the photographer. Eddie Stevens blundered noisily through the undergrowth and though his heart was thudding in his chest he felt a certain satisfaction as he heard the pursuers veer in his direction.

The light from the tractor headlamps was now far below them and the trees were thinning, but in the darkness the going underfoot had become treacherous, boggy and bramble-ridden. Eddie felt the water seeping through his town shoes and he cursed, but the men behind him were shouting to each other now, giving instructions, and he realized they knew the woods well and were hoping to cut him off. He ran on, bursting clear of the trees, and in the distance saw the curve of glittering lights that designated the roadway and houses above Rothbury Crags. Even as he did so, he was suddenly aware of the different textures beneath his feet, the springy tussocks of grass, and then the sliding, treacherous shale. He slowed uncertainly, aware of the manner in which the slope dropped away in front of him, and glanced back over his shoulder. Flashlights wavered among the trees and his heart was pounding. He hesitated, then turned away from the shale, began to scramble up the slope towards the dark shelter of a copse, wind-torn on the exposed hillside, and behind him someone shouted, a violent, angry sound in the darkness.

The going was rough, and rocks scored painful weals on his shins and destroyed his thin shoes. The breathing grew painful in his chest, lungs protesting, his ribcage sore with the unaccustomed effort of the flight in the darkness. He struggled on, hoping that the trees would give him some temporary cover, a screen behind which he could recover his breath and his sense of direction. Then suddenly, without warning, the rocks loomed up ahead of him, the slope fell away and he lost his balance, falling down the scarp slope, sideways, away from the copse on the hill, bouncing, rolling helplessly as bramble and stone tore at his clothing, and he let out an involuntary yell of pain and surprise.

He was brought up short, suddenly and agonizingly, as the craggy rock slammed into his chest, winding him, and he lay wheezing, breathless, the pain slashing through his chest, aware only of the sharpness of the night air in his lungs. He lay there, unable to move, watching the uncertain wavering lights on the ridge above him as men called to each other, questioningly. The searching gleams danced and hovered on the trees and the rocks and the ridge itself and Eddie Stevens lay still, gasping, waiting, scared. The lights faded momentarily, as the men moved away from the ridge and an eerie silence fell. It was broken by the rasping of boots on rock, a scrambling sound above him and then the light was bright and white, searing through the darkness, pinning him helplessly in its beam. A dark figure stood behind the light; heavy and menacing, it stood still for several seconds. There was a grunt of satisfaction.

'There you are. *Bastard.*'

Other lights joined the first, picked him out, then faded and died. The scrambling sounds increased and Eddie tried to struggle up. He got as far as his knees and crouched there, panting painfully. The pursuers were scrambling down the slope towards him but he was still breathless, unable to move, and afraid suddenly of the darkness at his back, the danger of the slope below, the unfamiliar territory of Rothbury Crags.

The men reached him; there were four of them, silent. They stood in a tight bunch staring at him for a little while and then one of them walked forward, slowly, as though the movement was something to savour and enjoy. A hand was wound roughly into Eddie's collar and he was jerked upright to his feet. There was a pause; Eddie waited, his nerves screaming and then the pain came as with a short, jabbing motion the man slammed his fist into Eddie's groin.

The next few minutes were hazy. He was aware of waves of pain, a numbness in his face, the salty taste of blood in his mouth and the panting, furious sound as the man who was kicking him gradually lost his rhythm and power. A rushing noise, the sound of wings, filled his head and he lost consciousness as his eyes seemed filled with blood, and the blackness turned red, then black once more.

* * *

There was the lightness of dawn in the sky. Every muscle in his body ached. He was aware of a distant rumble of sound, life stirring beyond Rothbury Crags. High above him in the glowing sky he could hear the thin keening of a predatory hawk, hovering for its morning kill. His tongue was swollen and thick and his senses reeled. Doggedly he sat up and looked about him. A rocky plateau, a thirtyfoot drop to a scattering of scree, rock and gorse. If he had fallen he might have been seriously injured . . . but the badger-hunters had themselves made a pretty good job of that. Eddie took a deep breath and knew when the pain lanced through his chest that a rib would have been badly bruised at best, probably splintered. But at the same time he felt a certain wry exaltation: he had drawn the pack away from the photographer and there would be a record of the night's doings. With his own brand of purple prose, he thought with satisfaction, the photographs of four startled men, three dogs and a badger would make a nice, lucrative little story.

The consideration gave him a sudden surge of strength and confidence. He tried to stand up. It was a mistake. He felt a swift dizziness descend upon him, his brain became turgid, dark images swam before his eyes and he lurched, fell sideways, and next moment was tumbling down the scree slope, torn at by gorse bushes, thudding along across small, painful outcrops that brought a scream of pain as the agony in his ribs extended through the range of his chest. Over and over he rolled, tumbling down the slope until he finally crashed into a thicket of gorse and the spines were in his flesh and he was sobbing, almost hysterically, among the shower of stones and dirt that still fell about him from the disturbed upper slopes.

After a few painful minutes he tried to sit up again, and after a further interval succeeded in rising to his knees. He looked about him. It was a matter of taking it carefully, waiting until he felt able to walk across the rest of the slope, towards the half-mile-distant road, where no doubt he would get a lift, even if his companion did not return to look for him. But no rushing, no more floods of dizziness and pain. Not after that fall. He turned back and looked up the slope to see how far he had fallen. And thoughts of height and measurement left him.

He was filled with a grim satisfaction, knowing now that it wasn't just the matter of a newspaper article — he intended getting his own back on those murderous thugs who had attacked him. But the thought flowed away from him as he stared up the slope and saw where the scree had broken and slid away, disturbed by his descent. Rock and small stones and earth had been disturbed, and there was something to be seen protruding from the shallow cavity to the left of the thick gorse. It was a piece of cloth. But there was something else too, something dark withered, discoloured.

Unsteadily Eddie Stevens walked forward, slipping on the loose scree, keeping his eyes fixed on the object in front of him and quelling the rising tide of excitement in his chest. He stood above the object, breathing in a manner shallow enough to avoid the stabbing pain from his ribs and only when he was sure did he lean forward, touch what he saw, tease it away a little from the earth. And then he was certain; positive that it was cloth, and discoloured bone, and withered skin and flesh; certain that he had stumbled upon something far more important than the illegal baiting of a badger in a Northumberland wood.

This, he knew, was a certainty for the nationals.

* * *

The office was small and unpretentious, located in one of the commercial buildings that had been built on the Quayside at the turn of the century. It was not exactly at the centre of the Newcastle business community, nor near the more fashionable premises inhabited by others of the legal fraternity in the city, but it suited Eric Ward, with its tall-ceilinged rooms, its echoing stairwell, the musty air of bygone business when shipping agents had jostled with merchantmen on the Quayside, seeking trade from the ships that lay thick in the Tyne.

There was a good view of the river from the narrow window in his own office, and he had had time since setting up on his own account to stare out of that window. His marriage to Anne had, of course, brought him a certain amount of business: he had walked the tightrope of pride on several of those accounts, aware they had come to him because of his marriage, and wanting to stand on his own two feet. Realism had eventually won over pride: he needed to re-establish himself in his own eyes as well as in those of the business community, and he knew also that once he'd been given the accounts he'd do as well with them as anyone else in practice along the Tyne — and better than some.

Even so, he had no intention of relying upon Anne's gentry connections, and he had steadfastly refused to have anything to do with the general commercial interests of the company she had established to manage her landed interests; anything, that is, other than the particular problem the company was facing right now, and which no local firm really had the expertise to deal with.

The matter would go to litigation, of course, and it was a good piece of business to have, but right now it was about the only piece of work available to him. He had employed two girls: Frances, to do the typing and general clerical work, and Lizzie who, in spite of the vaguely punk style she had recently adopted, yet managed to woo clients who had come to the office and who was also an extremely able and promising young legal executive. He had quizzed them both, carefully, upon how they felt about working in a Victorian building on the Quayside rather than a modern block near the city centre. Lizzie had summed it up: 'It's a gas, Mr Ward.' By that he had assumed she approved.

But right now he wasn't certain he had enough to keep them occupied. This week there had only been one new client and he hadn't even seen him yet. It didn't promise to be anything particularly interesting — and it meant a visit to the General Hospital. At least it could mean a walk in the sunshine.

He left the office at ten-thirty and walked along the Quayside, past the Custom House and Sandhill and crossed over beyond the Moot Hall to make his way behind the railway station and up the hill to Westgate. It was a fine, warm morning and the streets were bustling; whatever the recession had done to Tyneside it hadn't destroyed its sense of humour or its enjoyment of the city itself and he knew that it was a place he would never want to leave, even though it was a long drive from Sedleigh Hall, a drive he was still careful to make not more than a couple of times a week. The operation for glaucoma was still only six months behind him, and so far he was keeping the recurrence of symptoms at bay. He yet lacked the confidence to believe that his troubles in that direction were over, but at least he felt fit again, and the atropine he used was applied sparingly. It was marriage, rather than drugs, Anne insisted smugly, that had done the trick. He smiled to himself as he reached Summerhill: marriage might have helped his recovery from the operation and the traumatic experiences he had gone through at Shurrock's Drift, but it had certainly helped Anne Morcomb's confidence. She had matured remarkably in these few months: the girlishness had been replaced with a relaxed assurance. The status of a married woman appealed to her; and, oddly enough, it had increased her own commitment to the company that ran Morcomb Estates.

Eric Ward turned into the driveway of the General Hospital. He was sweating lightly from the climb up the hill: maybe he needed to get out more on the fells above Sedleigh Hall at weekends, or take up riding with Anne. He made his way through the swing doors marked *Inquiries* and was told that the person he wanted was in Redheugh Ward. A short walk along corridors painted with red, yellow and green lines, and he found himself standing in front of a bed where a young man of about thirty was lying, reading a local newspaper.

'Mr. Stevens?'

'That's me.'

'I'm Eric Ward.'

The young man laid aside his paper and looked at Ward with a certain curiosity. Eric returned the scrutiny. Stevens had been badly beaten, it seemed. His face was marked and cut, swellings and bruising around his eyes making his features seem grossly puffed, but his eyes were lively and humorous, his swollen lips clearly ready to break into an easy smile at the slightest provocation. They twitched now.

'Seen better stuff at the butcher's, hey, Mr. Ward?'

'You seem to have taken quite a pounding.'

'It was worth it,' Stevens replied and a glint of satisfaction came into his eyes. He raised a hand to scratch at his unruly thatch of hair and a grimace of pain twitched his mouth into a less happy state. 'I'm not so sure *all* the time, though.'

'Ribs?'

'Two. Cracked, not broken. But they play hell, for all that. Contusions, otherwise, I think that's the medical term. Oh, and a broken finger . . . see?' He waggled a plastered hand in Eric's direction in a vaguely obscene but comic gesture. 'Cuts down all *sorts* of activities on my part, you know? Can I get compensation for that, as well?'

Eric grinned, warming to the man. 'Depends whether you're right — or left-handed. Anyway, you want to bring charges of assault and battery, I take it, or malicious wounding—'

'What's the difference?'

'It'll depend upon the weapons used—'

'Boots, mainly.'

'. . . and the extent of the injuries—'

'I've told them you can have access to my medical records.'

'And you know who your assailants were?'

Stevens managed a grin and a chuckle. 'That's one thing about being a reporter and getting done over. The brethren, they got all the contacts you need, and the information comes rushing in. We don't like to see our own kind being done over, you know?'

'I gather they were local badger-hunters,' Eric said.

'That's right. You see, I work for the *Star* and there's been a fair bit of talk about the way country habits die hard even in the face of specific legislation. The nineteen eighty-one Act—'

'The Wild Life and Countryside Act.'

'You been doing your homework! The Act makes out a fine of up to a thousand pounds for hunting badgers, but the lads in the villages, they don't seem to be deterred. Wales, the West Country, Cheshire, Cumbria, Northumberland, they're all still rife with badger-baiting and killing, but what's more, there seems to be a kind of organized conspiracy to ignore it. The magistracy may be too close to the countryside themselves, a lot of them being landowners and all that, and they seem to impose ludicrous fines, sixty quid or something, even when the Act has been blatantly broken—'

'So it wasn't just badger-hunters you were after,' Eric suggested.

Stevens raised his unplastered hand and waved it doubtfully. 'Well, let's say there's more mileage in a bit of evidence that shows local corruption and that sort of thing. But while I *could* argue that, from the number of cases proceeded with in the courts and the fines that have been demanded, first I had to get hard evidence that the badger-baiting was still going on.'

'And you got it.'

'And some,' Stevens said ruefully, touching his puffy mouth gingerly. 'I'd managed to get some information from local farmers that there were setts above Rothbury Crags and that it was likely there'd be some digging up there fairly soon. In fact, I had to spend only two wasted nights up there before I got what I wanted — except I was a bit surprised when they came along with a tractor.'

'A *tractor*?'

'Oh, sophisticated stuff! Tractor to light up the scene, so they could enjoy it all that much more. The driver's called

Jack Henderson. He came armed with a steel probe: they use it to listen for movement in the tunnels dug by the badger. Then they had the dogs: the leader of the hunters is called Frank Penry, and he was the one with the "hard" dog.'

'How do you mean?' Eric asked.

'These teams, they always have one dog — this one was a black Patterdale — which has the job of going down into the sett. I gather they're special animals — powerful, fearless, usually scarred to hell from encounters with badgers, but with a jaw grip almost as fierce as the animal they attack. Then there's a back-up dog to which the men attach a collar with a radio device. It goes into the tunnel behind the "hard" dog, and they use a locater above ground, which buzzes, telling them where the tunnel runs and where the dogs have cornered the badger. Then they dig.'

'And this is *sport*?'

'So they say,' Stevens said with a grimace. 'Of course, they reckon they don't *kill* the badger, just *work* it.'

Eric shook his head. 'Hmm. All right, you have Frank Penry and Jack Henderson. There were four men.'

'Ian Timothy; Fred Jarvis. They were the others. A couple of reporters from the *Journal* came up with the names for me.'

'And you'll be wanting to press charges?'

'It's the name of the game. I think they went a bit over the top: I mean, they were taking their chances, but why lay into me the way they did? They could have killed me!' He hesitated then, thoughtfully, and his glance became glazed, as though he was thinking back to the morning at Rothbury Crags, turning over in his mind unpleasant possibilities.

Eric stood away from the bed, nodding. 'All right, I'll make a few inquiries of my own now, and I'll be in touch with you again shortly. When do you expect to leave hospital?'

'Tomorrow, probably. I think all the tests have been done now.'

'Well, call in to see me in a few days. I'll be able to give you a few dates by then for possible hearings, that sort of thing.' Eric hesitated. 'It couldn't have been a pleasant experience up there for you.'

Eddie Stevens tried to grin. 'It got the adrenalin pumping, I'll tell you that. But the rest of it.'

'You took quite a battering.'

'No, not just that. The body.'

Eric stared at him. 'I don't quite follow you.'

'The body. The corpse I found at the Crags. Didn't you read about it?'

'Rothbury Crags?' Eric frowned. 'Well, yes, I did read in the local paper that a body had been found in a shallow grave up at Rothbury Crags, but there wasn't much detail—'

'I got no byline.' Stevens grimaced.

'*You* found the body?'

'No one else. Sort of stumbled on it, if that's the right word when you fall over a cliff. It was just there, a hand stickin' out of the scree. I still have hopes of that story, but not while I'm stuck in here. That's why I'll be out, quick as I can.'

'The police haven't been able to identify the body yet?' Eric asked.

'They'll have their work cut out. I reckon the corpse was stuck in there more'n a year ago,' Stevens replied. 'They took it along to the forensic labs at Gosforth once they'd ferreted around at the Crags. But inevitably, they'll hit trouble in working out who the hell it was.'

'Man or woman?'

'Haven't heard, at this stage.' Stevens grinned again, painfully. 'But I'll find out. Reckon I got *some* rights to the story.'

Eric grinned back. 'I see what you mean. All right, I'll expect a call from you in a few days, when we can go over—'

'Hold on, don't rush away just yet.' Stevens stared at him, a hint of calculation in his eyes. He shifted to a more comfortable position in the bed. 'You . . . you're my lawyer now, right?'

'I suppose you could say that,' Eric replied, a hint of caution in his tone.

'Lawyers got their own kind of ethics, just like journalists.'

Erie could not avoid a smile. 'I think the emphasis is really the other way around. Lawyers are bound, as officers of the court—'

'Whereas journalists have a duty towards their public,' Stevens supplied. 'Okay, no matter, it's just that in a funny way we're tied up with the same kind of rules, like not talking about privileged matters, and all that jazz.'

'I suppose so.'

'It follows there's some things you wouldn't want to talk to me about.'

Eric Ward moved back towards the bed, curious. He sat on the edge of the bed, folded his arms and stared at the young reporter. 'Such as?'

'Morcomb Estates.'

Something moved unpleasantly in Eric Ward's chest. 'Morcomb Estates . . . they are a client of mine. But I can't imagine why the company should have any interest for you.'

Stevens caressed the swellings around his eyes and was silent for a moment. 'I heard about you, Mr Ward. You're becoming . . . shall we say, a character around Tyneside? A bit out of the ordinary run of stuffy solicitors. Maybe it's your background as a copper with the local force; maybe it's the physical trouble you've had — yes, I know all about the glaucoma. Or maybe it's the fact you managed to hook one of the best-heeled ladies in Northumberland — no offence meant.'

'None taken, Mr Stevens,' Eric said coolly. 'Yet.'

'Anyway, I heard of you.'

'And now you've retained me,' Eric said carefully. 'But what does Morcomb Estates have to do with anything?'

'Well . . .' Stevens paused, weighing his words carefully, but when they came, it was with a rush. 'It's not really Morcomb Estates at all. I know you're retained by them, and I have no interest in them, so much as what they're up to. I mean, I *know* you've got a reputation as a good, trustworthy lawyer and I know you'd not disclose to me any information that would come to you from a client, but the thing is, that kind of . . . *loyalty*, well, it wouldn't apply to anybody your client was acting *against*. Would it?'

'The word for what you're doing at the moment is, I am led to understand, Mr. Stevens, '*pussyfooting*.'

'I pride myself, Mr Ward, on being an investigative journalist.'

'So?'

'The badger-hunting thing, it's pretty small beer. For a long while I've been trying to work something up on a matter far bigger.'

'That's your problem. I don't see—'

'I picked you out to act for me over this assault charge because I wanted to get on your list, get to know you, and, frankly, I want to persuade you to trust me.'

'Why?'

'Because you act for Morcomb Estates, and the whisper is they'll shortly be suing Sheridan Enterprises, Inc.'

Eric stared at him in surprise. 'What possible interest can you have in such a case?'

'Not so much in the case itself. Rather, in whatever background information you might come across.'

Stiffly Eric said, 'There's no way I can talk to you about the affairs of Morcomb Estates, and as for Sheridan Enterprises, well, I can't see—'

'Aw, come *on*, Mr Ward, you surely must realize it's not Sheridan Enterprises I'm interested in as such. It's what's behind it all; it's *who's* behind the whole problem.'

'I'm not sure—' Eric began.

'Credit me with *some* sense! You know as well as I do! It's Lansley. That bloody conman, Halliday Arthur Lansley!'

* * *

The old city wall had been renovated at the foot of Westgate Hill, gardens had been laid out between the wall and the busy road that ran down towards Central Station, and on summer mornings like this the wooden seats were placed in what amounted to suntraps. Eric found a seat and sat back with his eyes closed and his head against the warm old stone. The sun was hot on his face, and the office could wait for another half-hour or so.

If he had had any sense he would not have come back into Newcastle, stubbornly to go about setting up a new practice when he could have lived the life of a country gentleman at Sedleigh Hall, tending the estates, keeping his legal senses alert by doing his stint on the Board of Anne's company, and undertaking the odd piece of business. She had tried to point out the nonsense of his trying to struggle back into a practice in his mid-forties. Dealing with little people, scruffy cases, earning a pittance when he didn't need to. But she missed the point: he *did* need to. It kept him alive, with a sense of purpose, and it helped persuade him he still *existed*.

Maybe it was something of the same kind of drive that had kept Halliday Arthur Lansley working when he could have taken his money and run years ago. He hadn't, and it had cost him dear. During the 'fifties he had entered the booming property market in a big way and had amassed groups of houses which he later demolished to turn into office blocks and business premises. Government pressures had brought the boom to an end for H. A. Lansley, but he kept wheeling and dealing deep into the 'sixties and then things had started to turn sour for him. There had been hints of prosecutions in the wind, suggestions of involvement with the shadier sides of northern business, and somehow his whole reputation had become tarnished, his name a byword for corruption. And eventually the prosecution had come: for tax evasion.

The reporter, Eddie Stevens, had looked into the whole matter with the assiduity of a blackbird looking for worms.

'I don't know how much you've investigated the whole business, Mr Ward, or how much you've read about Lansley, but believe me there's a whole lot of stuff you *can* learn from published sources, and a lot more from rumour. It makes little difference which project you turn over — Elderfield, the Comington Building, the new dock at Whitby, the offshore plant at Hartlepool — somewhere in there you'll find Lansley dealings, or Lansley money. I've looked, and it's amazing. But what really interested me was where the finance came for some of the projects.'

'He made a lot of money in the 'fifties and 'sixties,' Eric suggested.

'And lost most of it in that Elderfield Project, when the Ministry pulled the rug out from under him. No, Lansley had nothing more than a paper empire in the 'seventies, and yet he was still able to finance large projects, raise the banking for important contracts throughout the North. I just couldn't make out where it came from. And then I got the whisper.'

'What whisper?'

'Policemen are funny . . . well, you should know that. They usually keep their mouths buttoned tight, but whenever a case calls for outside experts, and particularly when people get drafted in from the Metropolitan Police, levels of resentment rise in the local forces and the rumours start to get about. I picked up the fringes of some of those rumours, and I began to make inquiries. And once you tell the fuzz you *know* something already, the fact is, they start to fill in some of the details for you.'

'And?'

'I got to hear of the North connection.'

'Drugs?'

'Just that.'

Eddie Stevens had sounded convincing. He had told Eric of the way addiction in Britain had grown, now to more than twenty thousand users. He told him of the Chinese connection centred on Gerrard Street in London, which had collapsed in a series of spectacular killings as the Triad gangs indulged in an inter-faction war that saw them lose their share of the opiate market. And he explained how the fall of the Shah of Iran had been the most significant event in the history of opiate addiction.

'Iran was the processing centre for years: raw morphine came in from Pakistan and was then shipped into the States and Europe. When the Shah fell the illegal chemists were chased out, but they simply crossed over into Pakistan, where were set up the processing centres for Europe — with a ready-made smuggling system direct into England.'

Addictive drug abuse, he pointed out, had been viewed as a London-based sociological hiccup which had by-passed the North, and while the jaded sons and daughters of the privileged had queued to shoot up in Chelsea the northern cities had seemed largely immune.

'But things changed: the rock groups gave drugs a sort of seedy glamour, heroin became classless, and with no jobs, problem housing and general no-hope attitudes, endemic in the North, the scene changed. It's become a serious problem in the North, Mr Ward. I saw a girl from Sunderland who shot Diconal into a vein by her groin and had to have her leg amputated; I've seen arms where the veins have disappeared, just long lines of scar tissue . . .'

'But what's all that got to do with Lansley?'

'The whisper is that when he got into serious financial trouble in the 'seventies he turned to the gangs, bought his way into the smuggling rackets, and began to use the profits from such illegal operations to finance the other projects to which he was already committed.'

'I've heard nothing of this before.'

Eddie Stevens had shaken his head vigorously. 'Nor will you, not openly. That's the whole point. Lansley, I'm told, was a middleman who kept most of his tracks well covered. But he was in on the system all right, raking off a profit for his other business. Then somewhere along the line a few rumours began to start, and the police always have their informers, as you well know. The trouble was, the police had no positive evidence . . . that, or else what hard evidence they picked up was suppressed.'

'Mr Stevens, I—'

'Please, hear me out. As I said, there's rumours. No hard facts. But what I *am* told is that there was a file which went up to the Director of Public Prosecutions, but the DPP backed off. Want of evidence. And then, in nineteen-seventy-eight, as you know, Lansley's empire collapsed, a few thousand shareholders found their money had vanished overnight, and fraud charges were brought against Halliday Arthur.'

'The charges were eventually dropped,' Eric demurred.

'But *why* were they dropped? Can I ask you this? Is it coincidence that just at the time when Lansley agreed to plead guilty to the charge of tax evasion there was a crackdown at Teesside Airport? You know how much heroin they found? It was worth, on the open market, a million and a half!'

'You're suggesting that had something to do with Lansley?'

'And there was Manchester. Two months later they got a big haul there, too. Dimorphine hydrochloride, in its white, crystalline state, was big business at Teesside and Manchester and once it hit the streets in the North as smack, harry, junk or whatever they wanted to call it, it made a lot of money for a lot of people.'

'And you seriously think Lansley was one of them?'

'I think he was, and I think he bought himself a slice of immunity from fraud charges in relation to his companies by turning in what he knew about shipments into Manchester and Teesside.'

'And the tax evasion charges on which he was finally convicted? How does that square with what you are saying?'

Blandly Eddie Stevens had said, 'Come on, Mr Ward, the police couldn't let him go completely scot-free! I think they scared him, told him they were prepared to take a chance on the charges, pushed him to agree a trade-off, but they still baulked at *complete* immunity. So in the end he settled for tax evasion.'

'He was sentenced to three years in gaol.'

'And was out within two,' Stevens scoffed.

'He had a heart condition, I understand.'

'Or a way into someone's bank account.'

'You're a cynic, Mr Stevens.'

'I'm a realist, Mr Ward.'

'And what precisely is it that you want from me?'

'Not a great deal, Mr Ward, not a great deal at all.'

Nor did it seem to be. Eric Ward rose, glanced about him and walked down from the green, back towards the office. At the Guildhall he had to wait a little while as traffic flowed busily past on the roundabout, heading for the Swing Bridge as heavy lorries thundered overhead across the Tyne Bridge, running south. There was a corvette, grey and sleek, moored on the Gateshead shore, and a Dutch freighter was unloading near Pandon. Eric leaned against the bollard on the Quayside for a few minutes, watching the activity, and thinking over what Eddie Stevens had said.

Background information, that's what he wanted. Nothing specific, but any background information that Eric might come across in the progress of the lawsuit that Morcomb Estates were bringing against Sheridan Enterprises, Inc. Eric himself had already stated his doubts to Stevens: it was unlikely that the Morcomb suit against the American firm would yield much information about Lansley, because the man's involvement in the matter had preceded the issues which now arose. It was true that in a sense Lansley had started the whole thing, and it was true that Eric Ward himself was due to interview Lansley in a few days' time, in order to obtain affidavits and ensure that the facts as they were now deposed were accurate. But it was all a far cry from heroin smuggling, and deals with Pakistani-based Iranians, and the sad, hopeless lives of young men and women in Byker, Gateshead and Wallsend.

The ethical situation was vague, of course. If the matter concerned Morcomb Estates, it was clear Eric was constrained to pass nothing to the reporter. But if it arose out of the lawsuit, and concerned the defendants, was there anything to prevent Eric passing it on? He sighed; it was uncertain. As an officer of the court there might be constraints, but it would really have to be a situation where he played it by ear. He'd have to make a judgment as facts emerged. *If* any useful facts emerged. He had, in any case, promised Eddie Stevens nothing.

He turned away from the river, crossed the road and made his way into the imposing Victorian entrance of the building in which he had his office. The familiar musty smell came to him and he smiled. He climbed the echoing stone stairs and began to hum to himself; he was suddenly imbued with a sense of wellbeing. He *had* been right to set up alone in business again. To return here this morning was to return to a satisfying, close existence, separate from Sedleigh Hall, which he loved, but equally home to him already.

Lizzie was at her desk in the small office to the right. He called in to her. 'Finished the Albright contract yet?'

'Yes, Mr Ward, and there's been a call from Selber and Sons. They want you to take over the property negotiations they've been undertaking on South Tyneside. Seems they're dissatisfied with the way things have been going with the London agents.'

'An appointment?'

'I suggested next week.'

'Good. You'll come with me.'

Lizzie glowed with pleasure. Ward entered the reception area. Frances was standing near the filing cabinet, a sheaf of papers in her hand. She smiled at Eric as he came in, but there was an edge of anxiety to it.

'Any messages, Frances?'

'No, Mr Ward. But there is a visitor.'

Eric glanced around the reception room in mock surprise. 'Couldn't wait . . . ?'

'It . . . it's a Mrs Crane.'

'And?'

'I . . . I showed her into your office.' When Eric stared at her in blank surprise she ran a nervous tongue over her lips. 'She said she knew you, Mr Ward. She said she'd rather wait in there and . . . and she said she was sure you wouldn't mind.'

'Mrs *Crane*? I don't know a Mrs Crane.' Exasperation had stained his tone, involuntarily, and the girl coloured. He raised a hand. 'All right, Frances, don't worry about it.'

He walked past, headed for the short flight of stairs that led to his office at the front of the building and opened the door.

The woman was standing at the window, looking out over the Quayside. He stared at her; she did not move for several seconds and then, slowly, almost casually, she turned and smiled at him. There was a momentary prickling at the back of his eyelids, the first signs of tension, and he stood stock still, aware that his mouth was foolishly open.

'Hello Eric. It's been a long time.'

It had been a *very* long time.

* * *

He could not now recall what colour her hair had been: there had been a time when she had, like many young girls, experimented. Now, it was a light brown, softly flecked with grey at the temples, a sign that she had used no artifice to retain her youth. Her body had thickened at the waistline but not to any great extent; rather, it had made her figure rounder, where she had always been somewhat lean. There was a hint of perfume in the room but it reminded him, oddly enough, of a day in the sunshine when the scent of dock leaves lay around them, on a headland in southern Ireland, when they had lain together in the long, sweet grass.

'*Sandra.*'

She smiled. 'Sandra *Crane*. You wouldn't have recognized the name.'

Eric stood there foolishly, wanting to touch her, make some gesture of welcome but afraid of the touch. There had been considerable bitterness, twenty years ago; it had all been washed away for her, no doubt, as it certainly had for him, but there remained the sensation of awkwardness, the inability to cope with a stranger who had been a friend and a lover and more.

'You're looking well.'

Perhaps she recognized the caution, the defensiveness in his tone, for she smiled again, and it held all the old confidence he remembered. Awkwardly he turned aside, made a vague gesture towards the easy chair placed in front of his desk and walked to the swivel chair he himself used.

'You're quite safe, Eric,' she mocked him. 'You don't *need* to get a desk between us.'

He sat down; after a moment's hesitation she followed his lead and took the easy chair, crossing one elegant leg over the other. She had always taken pride in her legs; he was suddenly nervous, and tense. 'This visit . . . it's a surprise, after all these years. I've heard nothing about you since it . . . ended.'

She cocked her head to one side, watching him. 'That's where we differ. I've heard a fair bit about you.'

'How?'

'Contacts here in Newcastle. I've come back from time to time. You'll remember I had friends out at Tynemouth; I came back for a marriage, for a funeral, that sort of thing. And, inevitably, talk got around to you. So I heard about your having to leave the police because of the glaucoma. It was bad?'

'Enough.'

'And I heard, the last time I was here, that you'd got . . . friendly with some young girl with acreage in Northumberland.'

'We got married recently.'

There were fine lines around her mouth and around her eyes: they suddenly became more apparent as her glance hardened. 'Wouldn't have expected it of you, really. Going for a young girl, I mean.'

'I don't see it's anyone's business but mine.'

The mocking smile came back. 'Just goes to show, doesn't it, Eric? We never could spend any time in each other's company, towards the end, without crossing swords. Still you're quite right. It's none of my business.' She paused, glanced around her at the sparsely furnished office, and raised a quizzical eyebrow. 'Even so, if she's loaded with money, how come you end up in this place? It's not exactly . . . well, I mean I'd heard you'd become a successful lawyer but is this the best way to persuade people they need to pay their bills? I would have thought the little wife would have helped out a bit.'

'This is *my* business, Sandra,' Eric said quietly. 'I owe it to no one, and I'll make my own way.'

She stared at him; he remembered how grey her eyes had seemed, years ago, but he had forgotten the strange flecks of green. She shook her head. 'It has been a long time. I thought that when I met you now I'd be meeting a stranger. You'd be far different from the man I knew and married; after all, people change in twenty years. I know I have. Yet I get the odd feeling you haven't changed that much. Older, greyer, carrying more weight — you used to be a skinny bastard, as I recall. But in some things you don't seem to have changed at all.'

'Such as?'

It was a mistake to ask the question; he knew it as soon as the words were out because something moved in her eyes, a feline calculation that disturbed him. She had always been more agile, mentally, than he, always able to keep one track, one argument, one point of view ahead of him.

'Such as your sense of independence; the deep-rooted pride you were always quick to reach for, like a cowboy going for a bloody gun.'

'Sandra—'

'It need never have happened, you know.'

'I don't think we should talk about—'

'We didn't talk about it at the time,' she insisted smoothly. 'What's the objection to discussing it now? After twenty years it's all so irrelevant that we ought to be able to look at the whole thing objectively.'

'That's the point. It is irrelevant. We've both moved on. So why talk about the past now?'

'Curiosity.' The corner of her mouth curled in satisfaction; she recognized his nervousness. 'You could have stopped it; all you need have done is beat the hell out of me.'

'What would that have proved?'

'That you cared, for God's sake.'

Would it really have been that simple?

She had been eighteen that summer, and already bored with being married to a policeman, bored with the long hours he was forced to keep, fractious when he returned home because she had been left alone, railing at him because he seemed unable to maintain the attitudes he had shown before they were married. He had certainly been at fault; he had failed to attach sufficient importance to the signs. Then subtly she had changed. There had been more mockery and less aggression; occasions when she had not been home when he returned but had only vague excuses for her absence. And then the occasion, the more horrifying for its very inevitability, when he had come home early one afternoon, unexpectedly, and had heard them upstairs.

He had stayed in the living-room for several minutes, cold, sweating, in a panic; then he had got control of himself and quietly he had climbed the stairs. The bedroom door had been left ajar. It was a warm afternoon. Their naked bodies had been sprawled across the bed, hers half covered by his. Eric had picked out small details: the rhythm of their movements, her fingers digging into the dark hair that matted the man's back, the gasping sounds that scarred the air. But the one detail that had scored into his memory as none other had been the sight of her face, against the man's shoulder.

Her mouth had been contorted with excitement, but it was an excitement generated not merely by the thrusting of her lover's body against hers. Her eyes were wide open, grey and green-flecked, and she was staring directly at Eric. She had deliberately left the bedroom door open; she might well have even heard Eric climbing the stairs. She had wanted him to see her like this, and as he stood in the doorway she made no attempt to warn the man with her, no attempt to break off the physical act. But more than that, it was what she was telling him as she glared at him: a mingling of challenge, fear and triumph. She wanted something to happen: she wanted noise and passion and excitement and terror but all he could do was to stand there, rooted to the spot, immobile and incapable of anything as his stomach turned to water and his hands trembled.

Her eyes had called to him, demanding to know what he intended to do about her.

He had turned away then, walked down the stairs, out into the sunshine of the warm afternoon. He had gone down to the river and had stood there for hours, staring at the black waters, and then he had returned home, to the semi-detached police house where he and Sandra had lived for such a short time. She had gone, taking her clothes with her. The marriage was ended, formally, a year later, and in the meanwhile they had met only twice, and barely spoken to each other.

He had *cared*, certainly. The problem was, a demonstration of that care had clearly been beyond him — at least, in the terms she would have wished.

'I was only using him, you know. To get at you.'

Eric shook his head. 'It really doesn't matter, Sandra. I think we went into the marriage blinded by things we thought were important—'

'Sex, you mean?'

'And the idea of marriage. Anyway, I wasn't the kind of husband you really wanted, or deserved, perhaps. I don't know, it's all so long ago.'

She smiled, lowering her eyelids in a mock demureness. 'I didn't stay with him, I can tell you that. Like I said, I just wanted you to get mad with me, show a bit of interest, you know? Anyway, after the divorce I got shot of him.'

'You married again.'

Her glance rose swiftly, and then her eyes were hooded again, but in a quick defensive movement. 'Yes, I married again. You . . . you stayed single a long time, didn't you?'

Eric shrugged. 'I didn't want to repeat the experience too quickly. And life in the force, it didn't really suit a regular situation. I got older, and then, well, the glaucoma, the reading for the Law Society examinations, and finally, setting up in practice, it all left very little time for thoughts of marriage.'

'Until the landed lady swept you off your feet, hey?'

Eric stared at her steadily. He didn't know why they were talking like this: there was the danger of old sores being reopened, and unnecessarily. Sandra and he had gone their separate ways; there was no need for them now to converge again. She wanted to hear about Anne, but he had no intention of telling her — not of the way he felt, not of the way he had resisted marriage until he was sure it was what Anne really wanted, not of the manner in which he had weighed in the balance his age, his illness, his possible dependence. 'It wasn't quite the way you suggest,' he said levelly. 'But look, I don't think we should go over all this. We seem to be . . . fencing. Your visit is a surprise. Why have you come to see me?'

'For help.'

She raised her chin slightly, as though issuing a challenge again, not the one that had been in her eyes that afternoon long ago, but one that demanded he recognize, in spite of all the years that had passed them by, that she could still have need of him.

'You've got a legal problem?'

'Not exactly.' She was silent for a little while, staring at the leather pad on his desk, frowning slightly as though she was trying to marshal scattered thoughts and images. 'I don't quite know where to begin, except to say maybe I needed to talk about you and me and the past, if only to get my own situation into perspective. I told you I dropped the man you caught me with.'

'After the divorce.'

'That's right. Well, after that I went a bit wild.' She wrinkled her nose, grinned a little mischievously, and shrugged. 'Hell, I was only twenty, and I felt like I'd just been released from some kind of prison. I don't mean to offend you, Eric, but well, I thought I needed to live it up a bit, you know? I went to London, got a job in one of the clubs and there was a . . . shall we say . . . a succession? I can't even remember their names now, but I really played the Queen Bee for a while. You could describe that as my red period.'

'And then?'

'I went into my blue period.' She grinned again, disarmingly. 'Young people can be so intense, can't they? So stupidly sure about things. And so committed to do what they think is right. The thing is, I suddenly threw it all over one night, the nightclub bit, and if I didn't exactly get religion, I sure got a bad case of conscience. I decided it was time I did something for people. I did just that, for four years.' She looked at him ruefully, and shook her head. 'I went into nursing, for God's sake. I mean, how unbalanced can a girl get?'

Eric was unable to restrain a smile. 'I'm not sure that demonstrates a lack of balance.'

'I, Sandra, the next-door whore?' This time she laughed; it was a laugh he remembered from sunny days. 'Well, don't get me wrong. Four years, I said: after that, Eve began to stir again and I thought it was time to make some of the hard work payoff. I took a job in the States for a couple of years, acting nursemaid to an old lady who was stiff with dollars and arthritis. When she paid her last dues I came back to England, then took a contract in Saudi — and believe me, that was an experience!'

'You seem to have travelled around.'

She nodded, and a hint of calculation crept back into her tone. 'It was out in Saudi that I first met Charles Crane.'

'The man you married?'

'That's right. Though it didn't happen then. He was working for an oil company as a junior executive and we had a brief fling, but it was several years later before I ran into him again, in London. We took it up again then, and after a while decided maybe we ought to get married.' She glanced at him, and checked for a moment. 'We talked quite a bit about it. It seemed a good idea at the time.'

'And now?'

'Well, that's the problem.'

'It's no longer a good idea? Sandra, I think I ought to tell you that I don't really go in for matrimonial matters. There are better solicitors on Tyneside who could handle this thing for you; besides, in view of our own relationship in the past I don't think it would be such a good idea if—'

'Hold on, Eric, I'm not asking you to handle a divorce case here.'

He frowned. 'So what is the problem?'

'I want you to find Charles for me.'

The room was silent for a while. Eric leaned back in his chair and stared at her. 'You've lost your husband?'

'That's right. Careless of me, isn't it?' Her laughter had a brittle, nervous edge and she was unable to meet his glance. 'But that's the fact. I don't know where he is.'

'I'm not sure that coming to me is the best way. The police—'

'Can't help. Or won't.'

'There are private inquiry agents—'

'I've tried two. They've drawn a blank.'

Eric scratched his cheek thoughtfully. 'How long has, your husband been missing?'

'Three years.'

'Three years?' Eric said incredulously. 'And there's no word from him?'

She hesitated, then shrugged. 'I think I'd better make it clear. I didn't exactly . . . look for him, the first two years or so. It's only recently . . .' She frowned, shook her head. 'Look, Eric, I know what you think about me; I know you'll never be able to get rid of the image I presented to you when our marriage broke up. You thought of me as a whore then, and I suppose you still do. Indeed, I've done nothing to change that impression by what I've been telling you in this office, have I?'

'I don't want to sit in any kind of judgment upon—'

'The fact is, I told you I've been through my periods — red, blue — and maybe I thought I was into a whole new one with Charles. I mean, we'd already known each other, he'd dropped out of the oil business but was pretty well-heeled, running his own business, and it seemed to both of us it could be pretty good.' She hesitated. 'Maybe it was, for a while. But then, somehow, it all fell apart.'

'How?'

'I don't exactly know. In a way, there were echoes of our marriage,' she said ruefully. 'He was away a lot, busy, preoccupied, and he seemed to be under some sort of pressure at the end. There had always been quarrels — you'll remember I could be pretty volatile at times. But some of them were bad, really tearing occasions when we just about took each other apart, verbally. The kind of quarrels I could never persuade you to enter.'

'What happened then?'

'It's difficult to pinpoint it. Our relationship deteriorated. We had no sex life; saw very little of each other; I became aware of his anxieties about something or other connected with the business — and then he just sort of disappeared.'

'He didn't tell you where he was going?'

'Not a word. Upped and left, that's all. Didn't even tell his partner where he was skipping to.'

'That was three years ago?'

'And I haven't seen him since.'

'Nor done anything about it.'

She sighed. 'All right, that may seem odd, but let's face facts. We had very little going for us, at the end. I hadn't been playing around, he was gone, it was no great loss, and his partner — Peter Stonier — he was pretty helpful when I went around and explained. There was some cash floating around in the business, and Peter let me have it as Charles's wife. Then I got a job, and I've been pretty comfortable, and I quite like living alone. So there was no need to go looking for Charles. If he'd wanted to skip, let him stay skipped. I had my pride.'

'So what's changed things now?'

Sandra hesitated, then rose and walked across to the window to look out over the Quayside. She was silent for almost a minute and he watched as she stood there. She seemed uneasy, nervous suddenly, unwilling to tell him the full story. Then she turned. 'Maybe I've changed. I think I have. You've just taken a chance, got married for the second time. Maybe you're sure it'll be no mistake. My second marriage was a mistake. I'm hoping my third won't be.'

'You're thinking of marriage again?'

She smiled defensively. 'Sucker for punishment, aren't I? But the fact is, I really think I could make it this time. I am different; I have settled — and I think I deserve the chance. I've been frank with you, Eric, and you've known me from a long time ago. The man I've now met is . . . different. He's good, and he'd be good for me. I want this marriage to work.'

Eric nodded, slightly embarrassed suddenly. He had no right to question her motivation, nor to concern himself with the wisdom of her actions. 'It isn't strictly necessary that you find Charles Crane, of course. If it's a question of ending the marriage, the separation of three years, the desertion on his part—'

'No, I need to know where he is.'

'Why?'

'I don't want a new marriage to start off on a wrong footing. I don't want Charles suddenly turning up some day from God knows where and spoiling things. He can be a bastard when he wants to be,' she added grimly, 'and there are maybe things he could say . . . I want to find him, talk to him first, before I go through with another marriage.'

There was something wrong with the words; they had been prepared, she had thought them out but they lacked conviction and Eric was puzzled. She looked at him suddenly, and perhaps she sensed his puzzlement. She was oddly pale and she came back towards the desk and sat down.

'I think there's something else,' Eric said quietly.

'I . . . I suppose there is. Oh, don't get me wrong, I wouldn't like him coming back, trying to spoil things, but I reckon I could stop that. He's been no angel himself, and there were deals he entered into when he was out in Saudi, well, they wouldn't stand the light of day too well, even if they were a long time ago.'

'So?'

'So I want you to find him . . . so I can be persuaded he can be found.'

'I don't understand.'

'When he disappeared . . . Eric, it was all so *complete*. I mean, there's been nothing, nothing at all!'

'What are you trying to say?'

There was a certain wildness in her glance, as though she was scared by the words tumbling over in her mind. 'There's been no word; no letter; no call; no report. It's as though he's vanished off the face of the earth. But, you see, I can still remember the way he behaved before he left — the anxiety, the tension. He was always a man who was . . . into deals, maybe a bit shady, I don't know, I didn't ask, but when he disappeared like that—'

Slowly Eric said, 'You think I won't be able to find him.'

She stared at him. She touched her dry lips with her hand.

'You think he's dead.'

Her hand touched her mouth. 'I . . . I think there is that possibility.'

Eric considered the matter for a little while, then shook his head. 'I don't think this is necessary, and I don't think it's my scene at all. It's the police I should recommend to you; it's their line of business.'

'I have nothing to take to the police. Besides, what if he was involved in something shady? My friend, the man I want to marry—'

'You said you wanted the marriage to start right, Sandra. If you keep anything from him, it could be a bad start. No, I think it would be better if you left it all alone; get your divorce, get remarried, forget all about Charles Crane. Put it all behind you. Make your new start.'

'It's not quite as simple as that!' she flashed at him. 'It's all very well for you — married to the landed gentry!'

Eric flushed. 'I don't see—'

'The fact is, the man I want to marry, he's good and he'll look after me, but . . . he hasn't much money, and some months ago he was made redundant at the firm he works for. Life won't be all that easy for us, and I don't want it spoiled in that way.'

'Go on.'

'I want you to find Charles. And if you can't find him, I want you to act as my legal adviser.'

Eric stared at his hands. 'There's an insurance policy,' he said flatly.

'That's right!' Anger marked her tone, and she spoke more quickly, the words rushing out, almost tumbling over each other. 'I knew nothing about it. When the bastard left me there was a little cash, but I didn't know about the policy until a few months back, when I was turning out old things and found it hidden at the back of the bloody wardrobe! He took out a policy on his life seven years ago. The premiums were paid up until the time he left me. Do you know how much would come to me if that policy matures? *Thirty-five thousand pounds*!'

He looked up at her; there was a hint of tears in her grey, disturbed eyes.

'Sandra—'

'Don't you understand what that money could mean to us? We could get a start, buy a small business!' She stood up, hands clenched together, and glared at him defiantly. 'Are you going to tell me I don't *deserve* a new start?'

* * *

After Sandra had gone Eric looked again at the snapshot of Charles Crane that she had left with him. It was a colour photograph but the definition was not good: she had told Eric it was the only one she had since Charles Crane had always displayed a marked reluctance to having his photograph taken. The snapshot showed a fair-haired man who looked to be in his mid-forties; he was wearing an open-necked shirt and a sports jacket with grey trousers, and was leaning against a car outside what appeared to be business premises of some kind. The sunlight had made him squint somewhat, distorting his features, but Eric guessed that if he were to meet him he would probably be able to recognize him, with his high cheekbones and wide mouth.

Eric opened a new file cover and slipped the photograph into it, then placed the file cover in his drawer. He rose and walked across to the window to look down to the afternoon Quayside. There were a number of people strolling about, enjoying the sunshine, watching the activity on the Dutch freighter, while across the river the corvette seemed to be making preparations for departure.

As he stood watching, Eric observed Sandra crossing the road to the Quayside. She walked along the quay for a few yards and then stood gazing at the corvette for several minutes. Then, uncertainly, she turned and began to walk towards Pandon.

Eric watched her go. He was still not certain he was right in agreeing to help her. Finding errant husbands was a bit out of his line; on the other hand he felt somewhat sorry for her. She had lost her way early in life: their marriage had never been right for either of them and in a way her defiant adultery had been a good thing, in bringing to an early end a relationship that would have scarred them more deeply had it lasted longer. Now they were sufficiently distant from those days to ignore what had happened; the scars had healed, and Eric even felt there was a certain warmth, a friendship growing between them. Once she had got over the outburst over the insurance policy she had calmed, and they had talked, she'd shown him the photograph of Charles Crane and at last, reluctantly, Eric had agreed to do what he could for her.

If he were completely honest with himself he would be forced to admit that Sandra might be twenty years older than when he had known her, but she had still retained the sense of humour he had enjoyed in those days, and she was still an attractive woman.

He was not alone in thinking so, either. He was vaguely amused when he saw the man in the sweater and dark blue jeans stroll along some thirty yards behind Sandra, making her way towards the far end of the Quayside. He had been leaning on the rail, casually watching the Dutch freighter operations, but Eric had noted the way his head had turned when Sandra had passed him. After a few moments he had run a hand through his springy black hair and then straightened, turned to walk a short distance behind Sandra, obviously admiring her figure, and the swing of her walk. She had always had the capacity to turn heads, and she had obviously not lost it.

Eric watched as Sandra reached the end of the road and crossed behind a parked lorry before making her way towards the steps that would lead her up towards the Castle. Her admirer also disappeared in that direction, while retaining a regulation thirty yards or so. He was obviously biding his time, choosing his moment to make the approach. Eric wondered whether Sandra had changed enough to repel the approach, then was vaguely annoyed at his own lack of mental charity.

Besides, he had other things to think about. He was due that evening for a conference with Anne and the company secretary of Morcomb Enterprises, for the necessary briefing before he interviewed the man Eddie Stevens was so interested in: Halliday Arthur Lansley.

CHAPTER 2

'Who?' Anne demanded.

He had tried to explain that her surprise was no greater than his had been when he had walked into his office and found Sandra waiting there, but whereas he had quickly recovered from that surprise, things seemed different for Anne. He had showered at the flat in Newcastle, changed, and when he emerged into the sitting-room he found her standing with a gin and tonic in her hand, staring out over the darkening city, her back displaying a rigidity that suggested tension.

'But what did she really *want*?'

'I told you: she wanted me to help find her husband.'

'It seems such an odd request. I mean, after all these years . . . And why you?'

Eric stood beside her. Their arms touched lightly. He remembered the first time they had made love, and he recalled the nights when they had lived together at Sedleigh Hall, after his operation and before they were married. She had developed a new sense of security since then, an inner calm that increased her attraction for him: she had become more assured since her marriage, and he loved her. But tonight some of her insecurity had returned, merely at the sound of his ex-wife's name.

She could still seem very young at times.

'I don't understand why you're so eager to help her, Eric.'

'I would have described my attitude as reluctant, rather than enthusiastic.'

'But you're still going to help her.'

'I felt sorry for her.'

Anne knew there was more to it than that; the knowledge was there in the continued tension that lay between them. But there was no way in which he could explain satisfactorily to her — at least not without increasing her insecurity even more. It was rooted in only half-understood emotions within himself: a perhaps misplaced sense of loyalty towards Sandra in spite of what had happened and all the time that had passed; a feeling that he still owed her something for the golden days when they had both been young; the need to demonstrate to himself that he could bury all the hurts and behave rationally and sensitively towards the woman who had at one time torn his emotions apart and shattered his ego in the worst possible way. He was aware that Anne was suffering from an uneasy suspicion that she herself could not explain, but for now they would both have to come to terms with their inability to communicate private thoughts to each other. It was a pity, so early in their marriage.

'I mean, you've steadfastly refused to help *me*,' Anne said almost petulantly, 'by taking over the legal side of Morcomb Estates. You know we've been having trouble keeping things on the rails—'

'Your solicitor is elderly, and maybe a bit slow, but still efficient,' Eric interrupted. 'And we've had all this out so many times. I simply can't accept working for your company: I have to make my own way, you know that. It's stupid, maybe; chauvinistic; male arrogance — but that's the way it is.'

She looked at him suddenly, her eyes dark with subdued resentment. Then she sipped her drink, and shook her head. '*Pig!*' she said, with a note of satisfaction in her voice.

Eric smiled, recognizing a corner had been turned. 'Besides, I *am* helping you, with this Lansley thing. What time is Carson joining us?'

'The pompous company secretary of Morcomb Estates announced he would be joining us at eight and, knowing the man as I do, I am certain he will ring the doorbell with not more than thirty seconds to go before the appointed hour.'

She was right.

* * *

Patrick Carson always dressed in tweeds during the evenings; his uniform for business meetings during the days was a grey flannel suit. He was small, plump and fifty, with flyaway eyebrows, thick, bushy hair that was pepper-and-salt in colour and thin wire in texture, and he was addicted to Irish jokes, mainly because he still retained a hint of an Irish brogue even though he had been brought to Tyneside when he was a mere child. Now, as he accepted a whisky from Eric, he waved a hand expansively and announced he had had a trying day.

'What's been the problem?' Eric asked.

'Oh, that damned Sinclair firm. They've made a complete botch of the Cumbrian business and I was so mad after three hours' discussion that I gave Sinclair the biggest bawling out you can imagine. He went purple as Northumberland heather.' Carson's eyes twinkled and he sipped at his whisky. 'I told him if he wanted satisfaction I'd give it to him, of course. But it would have to be an Irish duel — swords at twenty paces.'

Eric chuckled and sat down beside Anne. 'You sure you weren't hard on him? That Cumbrian contract is a difficult one.'

'Ah,' the little man snorted, 'that's not the point! It's the long-winded way he goes about things! I tell you, let's just hope he never gets asked to launch a ship. *His* way would be to get someone to hold the bottle of champagne and then get five hundred people to throw the ship at it!'

Anne laughed and leaned forward, tapped him on his knee. 'All right, all right, but we're not here to discuss the Cumbrian business. Have you been able to prepare the papers for the Sheridan suit?'

'Ah yes, indeed.' Carson sipped at his whisky again, then turned to pick up his briefcase. He drew it onto the settee beside him, clicked open the lock and withdrew a slim, embossed file with Morcomb Estates printed on the cover. 'I have it all here: burned more than a bit of midnight oil on this, Eric, but I'm glad you're taking it on. If we'd left it to that old dodderer . . .'

Anne shifted slightly beside Eric and glanced at him. 'The fact is we *have* persuaded Eric—'

'Quite so, quite so,' Carson said hurriedly. 'Now, do you want me to go through the file in detail with you?'

'I think a brief rundown on what you see as the problem would be useful, Patrick. The detail is something I can get down to later.'

'Okay, Eric, I'll keep it as short as possible.' He opened the file and glanced through the separate sheets for a few moments, then nodded. 'Right, the briefing for the hearing is all here: the hearing is due in about six weeks' time for the preliminaries and no doubt you'll want to consider which counsel you'll advise to act for us.'

'I'll need to see the papers. There are horses for courses.'

'That's right. Well, the basic issues are these. Sheridan Enterprises, Inc. are the present owners of the El Centro estate in Mexico. The property is about sixty miles east of the Colorado River; it was purchased by the company some five years ago. At the time of the purchase, it was made subject to a legal charge in favour of Halliday Arthur Lansley—'

'Can you just hold on a minute?' Anne grimaced wryly. 'I know you did try to explain this legal charge business to me but I didn't get it too clear then, and I'm about to get confused again—'

'It's simple enough, really,' Eric explained. 'When some property or land is sold, it's possible that the seller owes money to a third party. To protect himself, the third party might have made the debt a charge on the land.'

'Which means—?'

'It means that the *buyer* of the land will take the land subject to the charge; that is, he is obliged to pay over the amount of the debt to the third party before he hands over the rest of the purchase price to the seller.'

'And if he doesn't?'

'He'll be liable personally to the third party. The land remains burdened with the debt.'

Anne frowned. 'But what if he didn't know of the existence of the debt in the first place?'

'Ah, well, in normal circumstances the third party will have protected himself by *registering* the charge in accordance with local law. Once the charge is registered, it's binding on the purchaser of the land whether he *actually* knew of it or not.'

'Hmmm . . .' Anne said doubtfully.

Eric smiled. 'Think of the mortgage system. The bank lends you money to buy some property. That property is then *charged* with the mortgage. If you sell the property to me, I then have to payoff the mortgage money and give only what's left of the purchase price to you.'

'Can we get on?' Carson asked in a pained tone.

Eric laughed, and nodded. 'All right. You said the El Centro property was made subject to a legal charge—'

'In favour of Halliday Arthur Lansley. That charge was later made over to Morcomb Estates, by Lansley.'

'What was the nature of the transaction?' Eric asked.

Anne pulled a face. 'It was some three years ago when he was in deep trouble. You'll remember he was hauled up for various fraud charges and was eventually sent to prison. Well, shortly before that we had a problem: he had undertaken certain share transactions for Morcomb Estates in connection with land in Northumberland. The idea was to develop the land for rough shooting and Lansley — who did a lot of business with my father before he died — was deeply involved with this scheme before doubts about his financial security came to light. At that time, and with rumours of police investigations beginning to filter through, we were advised to nail Lansley for the cash he owed us before things really blew up in his face.'

'So you nailed him?'

Anne grunted in unladylike fashion. 'As far as it was possible to nail him.'

'The man should have been an Irishman,' Carson said. 'He's got the luck of the Irish. He's the kind who could kidnap a boy, send him home to collect the ransom, and the father would send the kid back with the money.'

'We got some of the shares sorted out,' Anne went on, 'and there were two tracts of land in Northumberland we were able to accept in satisfaction of a large part of the money owed us by Lansley. But then he declared himself unable to transfer any more assets—'

'The company put pressure on him—'

'And he came up with the El Centro deal.'

'That's right.' Patrick Carson scratched his ear thoughtfully. 'Don't get it wrong; we looked pretty carefully into the whole thing. I mean, it's not all that usual to sanction a transaction like this in satisfaction of a debt. I even flew out at the company's behest to have a look at the property. You never know, do you? I mean, Lansley could have been trying to sell us a pup. No. the property's there all right, it holds a housing complex; it's worth a good few million dollars, and if the charge held over it was valid, then transfer of the charge would have been a sound enough cover for the debt owed to us by Lansley.'

'And was the charge valid?'

'Sound as a bell. Checked at the downtown offices. The charge was validly registered in nineteen-seventy-four. So we went ahead with the transfer.'

'And?'

'When Lansley got into real deep water and found himself heading for gaol he got rid of quite a lot of his holdings. One of the properties I'd seen in Mexico, owned by him, was sold to Sheridan Enterprises, Inc. They were picking up quite a lot of land in that area. It's a development company, and it's pretty big. But cagey. Anyway, once Lansley got put away for three years, we thought we'd better recover our money by offering to give up the charge over El Centro. Sheridan Enterprises weren't interested, and there the matter lay for a while.

'You didn't pursue it?'

Carson wriggled a little, suddenly uncomfortable. 'Didn't seem necessary. I mean, it was *safe*, there was no reason to worry, and the moment Sheridan Enterprises tried to transfer the property we could step in and demand as much of the purchase price as was necessary to cover our charge.'

'So you were simply waiting for a transaction to take place regarding the land?' Eric asked.

'Right; then we'd swoop in like an Irish canary.' Carson paused. 'The transaction finally came on last May.'

'Sheridan Enterprises tried to sell the land?'

'Right. We got notice, put in our claim — and the bastards suddenly screamed that we had no rights in the land at all!'

Eric stared at him for a few moments. 'What argument did they raise?'

'None.'

'How do you mean?'

Carson's cheeks were pink and his eyes evasive. He shrugged. 'They just denied liability.'

'So what happened then?'

'That's where we're at, at this moment.'

Eric was silent for a little while. He watched Anne as she rose and walked across the room to pour herself another gin and tonic. 'What do we know about Sheridan Enterprises?' he asked.

Carson sighed. 'By all accounts, not much.'

'They've been, shall we say, somewhat terse in their dealings with us,' Anne added as she sat down beside Eric again.

'And how much money is involved in the legal charge?'

Carson handed the file across to Eric wordlessly. It was open; the sheet that was exposed consisted of the registered charge on the El Centro estate. It was in the sum of eighty thousand dollars.

'We think the key lies with Mr Lansley,' Carson said. 'The first step is to be certain that he endorses the claim we make regarding the charge. If he refuses to do so, or fails to show the transaction with Sheridan Enterprises was watertight, then we think we can proceed against him for fraud.'

'There might not be much mileage in that,' Eric murmured. 'He could have lost most of what he had when he was gaoled.'

'If we can't proceed against *him*,' Anne said, 'it looks as though we'll have to fight Sheridan Enterprises. So, as Patrick says, the key really lies with this man Lansley.'

'And as for his possessing assets,' Carson added, 'well, you'll be able to tell us more after you've seen him, but the story is that he seemed to come out rather well from his financial ordeals and prison term. He presently lives in the south of France.'

* * *

They did not stay up late. Once Carson had left them, Eric spent a little while reading the contents of the file and then he joined Anne in bed. She was sleepy, but when he caressed her she turned, murmured something, and they made love, quietly and gently. Later, as she lay in his arms she snuggled her head into the curve of his neck and muttered, 'Still don't see why you have to help that bitch.'

'It was a long time ago, Anne.'

'All the more reason.'

'All the more reason not to dredge up old battles. She needs help.'

'Mmmm. Suppose so. Anyway, you concentrate on this El Centro deal for me. Won't give you much time to go chasing around with ex-wives.' She was silent for a little while and from the regularity of her breathing he thought she had gone to sleep. Then she said, with a surprising vehemence. 'You know, it's just not right!'

'What?'

'That bloody man Lansley. One of the biggest fiddlers in the country; he cons all sorts of people; he gets gaoled for fraud, and is guilty of the Lord knows what else.'

Eric thought for a moment of the comments Eddie Stevens had made about Lansley, but kept his counsel.

'And what happens at the end of it all?' Anne challenged. 'Okay, he gets a prison term, but *that's* cut short because he's supposed to be ill, and then he ends up in the sun, in the south of France, living, by all accounts, like some seraglio owner. It's just not right!'

She kissed his chin, and settled down more deeply in the bed. 'The bastard,' she said. 'He's the kind of character who could get away with murder.'

* * *

The road Eric Ward picked up south of Gateshead had been much improved. The dual carriageway swept through the east Durham countryside with views of a blue-black sea to his left and the lifting hills of Cleveland ahead of him. A new motorway had been constructed at Middlesbrough so he saw little of the town as he drove above it, heading past the tangle of streets and the threatened chemical and steel works that had once promised to make the town the most prosperous in the North-East. He passed the Tontine, with the ancient mined peak of Roseberry Topping pointing its sharp finger to the sky, and then he settled into the long, smooth drive along the carriageway that took him through the Cleveland Hills, slicing past the white horse cut in the chalk, skirting the grand sweep of coastline thrusting south with its hamlets and small fishing villages he had visited as a boy.

An hour's drive out of York he stopped at a small hotel and managed to coax a pot of coffee from the receptionist:

it was far preferable to struggling into some tourist tea-shop. As he sat in the deep armchair of the hotel lounge he mulled over the reason for his drive to York. Sandra had been so vague in her story; there had been so little to go on, so few leads to follow that it seemed logical to start with the place where Charles Crane had last been seen by his wife, three years ago.

'I'd gone along to the business,' Sandra had told him. 'He'd been away for a couple of days, and I needed to see him but when I arrived he seemed less than pleased to see me. We had a bit of an argument, in fact, and in front of Peter Stonier, his partner, too. I stormed out — you'll recall I always had a bit of a temper myself. And that was the last I saw of him.'

'He didn't return, to pick up his clothes, other possessions, from the house?'

'He had very little there,' Sandra had explained. 'As I told you, he was away a lot, and I know for a time he'd rented a flat up near Tyneside, or somewhere. It's a long time ago really; you can forget a lot in three years.' She had stared at him, an odd look in her eyes. 'You can forget more in three than you can in twenty. Or maybe it's just that there are some things you never really want to forget.'

Hastily Eric had said, 'All right, so you had this quarrel, and he still didn't return home. But did you have *no* idea where he had gone?'

She shrugged. 'I was mad with him; I didn't inquire. I think I did ring Peter Stonier after a few days, but he was kind of vague too. He said as far as he knew Charles was away trying to sharpen up some contacts: the business, he admitted, wasn't going too well, and anything Charles could do to help was all right with him.'

'Who had he gone to see?'

'I tell you, I don't know. Peter didn't say, or didn't know, and I was so fed up I couldn't care less. Then, finally, Peter rang to tell me he'd heard nothing from Charles and was getting worried. Creditors were pressing.'

'Did you start looking for your husband then?'

'No. Criticize me if you like but I just stayed home, kept my head down and smoked more than a few cigarettes. Until Peter finally came around to see me.'

He had been a worried man. He had had time in Charles Crane's absence to spend more than a few hours with the company books and while there was no evidence that Crane had been defrauding his partner, it was clear that the level of expenses Charles Crane had been drawing on the business was too high for the company itself to afford — if business was not flowing in. And the reverse had been true: there were outgoings in plenty, but very little by way of income.

'He was very nice about it,' Sandra said. 'He told me the firm was in deep trouble, and if he was to get out of it with anything at all he was going to have to liquidate all the assets right away. The trouble was, while Charles, as his partner, wasn't around to be consulted — and Peter asked me if I knew where he was — things were difficult.'

'You told him you had no idea where your husband had gone?'

'That's right. I don't think he believed me at first, but eventually he went away and said he'd be talking to a solicitor about how best to settle the whole matter. In the event, he rang me a week or so later to say he'd been able to negotiate the lease, make it over to someone else, sell off the stock and come out with a little cash after all. He told me it wasn't much but as Charles's wife, it was only right that I should have it. If Charles came back, well, that was between Charles and me. As far as Peter Stonier was concerned, I was entitled to what was left.'

'How much was there?'

'Not much. About two thousand, I seem to recall.' Her glance became vague, as she thought back, and a hint of a smile touched her lips. 'He brought the money around. It was in cash. Maybe he had done some sort of fiddle himself, avoiding tax, that sort of thing, you know what I mean. Or maybe it was in cash because he thought the sight of so many notes would kind of impress me. I think he'd have liked to make a pass, you know? I think he was . . . *interested*, and with Charles making a run for it like that . . .' She shrugged, shook her head. 'He didn't summon up the courage, in the end, and off he went, and that was the last I saw of him.'

'He left the area?'

'Eric, I really don't know.'

They had been living in a house in Guisborough, but the business had been based in York, although it seemed Charles Crane had travelled fairly extensively throughout the North-East in his attempts to drum up business. York seemed a good enough place to start: the house in Guisborough had long since been sold and, heavily mortgaged, had brought in very little for Sandra to live on.

'But if the house was sold, wasn't your husband's signature necessary on the conveyance?'

She shook her head. 'No, the house had always been in my name, even though he paid off the premiums. Funny, that . . . maybe there had been a streak of something good in him all along. Leaving me something to live on. Perhaps it was that he always guessed he would be walking out on me some day . . .'

* * *

Eric parked in the compound behind the old town wall that encircled the city and made his way first towards the massive structure of the cathedral, still buttressed by thick timbers where excavations in the foundations were being carried on, and then walked slowly along halfforgotten streets, tiny shops, pedestrian precincts of the university town, until he came to the Shambles. The mediaeval street was thronged as always, and he was tempted to browse along it, past the old bookshops and art and craft shops, but resisted it: the address Sandra had given him was five minutes' walk away and he did not want to spend too much time in the town before he returned to Northumberland. Anne had been cool enough about his visit to York as it was, although she had insisted that her concern was rooted in her anxiety that he would find the long drive too tiring, and a strain upon his eyes. He had promised he would get back as quickly as possible.

When he finally reached the address Sandra had given him he was surprised. He had expected business premises; instead, as the roadway narrowed and then petered out, he was faced by a gravelled yard in which several vehicles were parked and then a long low building fronted by a small showroom. The sign over the door proclaimed: WAVERLEY BUILDERS LTD. Eric entered the showroom and a young, fair-haired girl popped her head up from behind a counter.

'Be with you in a minute!'

'It's all right.' Eric looked about him. The showroom was laid out with do-it-yourself materials: clearly, whatever the sign might proclaim, a sideline was being developed out of which Waverley Builders would get little or no building work themselves. Or maybe it was a way of getting business: when the enthusiastic amateur botched the job he'd come back to Waverley to put it right.

'Sorry to keep you waiting, sir. Can I help?'

She had a freckled, pug-nosed face and smiling blue eyes.

'You been working here long?' Eric asked.

She was slightly taken aback. 'Since we started. I came here straight out of school. It's my dad's business.'

'Is your father here at the moment?'

'He's in the office. Is it him you want to see? He's pretty busy,' she said doubtfully.

'I won't take up much of his time,' Eric replied.

'It's not a complaint, is it?'

He smiled and shook his head. 'Tell him Mr Ward would like a few minutes with him.'

She hurried through the door at the back of the showroom and Eric waited for several minutes. The man who finally came into the room was a rougher, older version of the daughter: thinning sandy hair, dark freckles, a spreading pug nose and a suspicious mouth. 'I'm Fred Waverley. You wanted to see me?'

'I'm sorry to bother you. My name's Ward: I'm a solicitor from Newcastle.'

'Don't care to have too much truck with lawyers.'

'It's a common enough attitude, Mr Waverley, and an understandable one. But I'm making some inquiries—'

'If it's about that business with young Skinner, I got a witness,' Waverley interrupted, 'who'll swear that—'

'My inquiries don't concern you or your business,' Eric said quickly as he recognized the taciturnity that could develop into silence. 'You bought the lease of these premises some three or so years ago, didn't you?'

Waverly sniffed thoughtfully and drew suspicious eyebrows together like a barrier against doubt. 'All straight and above board, that was.'

'From whom did you obtain the lease?'

'Solicitors in York arranged it. The business was closing down. Got the lease for a song, all right, I admit that, but the whole place was a mess. Needed to knock down part of the building, leave the yard open for lorries, rebuild the office section, so it wasn't all profit, believe me. Took us a year to get straight. But it's the kind of place for a building business.'

'And the man who assigned the lease to you?' Eric persisted.

Fred Waverley shrugged, turned away, and leaned against the counter, watching his daughter for a few moments as she rearranged various items on the tool rack. Then he nodded. 'Stonier,' he said. 'He was called Stonier.'

'Did you have much to do with him or his partner?'

'Partner?'

'Charles Crane.'

'No. Never heard of him. Never even saw Stonier, for that matter. I was looking for some property, this came on the market, I snapped it up. You trying to tell me now that there was something wrong with the lease? You better see them lawyers in York — far as I know it was all straight.'

'No, that's not the way of it,' Eric reassured him. 'The fact is I'm making inquiries about the whereabouts of Mr Crane.'

'Skipped it, did he?' Waverley grunted.

Eric paused, eyed the man thoughtfully for a moment. 'Why do you ask that?'

Waverley shrugged. 'Instinct.'

'I don't understand.'

Waverley scratched his nose, looked about him with an air of quiet satisfaction, and sniffed. 'I tell you, people look down on the building trade. Some reckon we're just a set of cowboys, blokes who are out to make a quick bundle and then off again. I've heard 'em, they talk about the number of bankruptcies in the trade, they talk about the fiddles, the tax dodges, the casual labour who drift from job to job and don't pay no taxes . . . All right, there's plenty of moonlighting, and the fiddles that happen on site, well, I know all about that as well, but if you really want to make your money in this business, steady, year in, year out, it's to be done on a regular basis. That's the kind of operation Waverley Builders is. Steady, reliable, and no fiddling.'

'I've no doubt, but—'

'You ask me why I guess that this chap — Crane? — why I guess he skipped? All right, you come making inquiries; it means you can't find him; that means a little piece of jigsaw clicks in my brain from the time I picked up this lease. Told you, got it for a song. But when I got here, I was surprised. Or maybe not surprised. Not really sure.'

'I don't understand.'

'The place was a mess,' Waverley said disgustedly. 'I mean, I had my doubts from the beginning. Who in their right minds would open up a carpet sales business this end of the city? There was no parking here then: I laid out that yard. The buildings were unsuitable and the location wrong. There'd be no customers coming down here — so maybe they were wholesale dealers? Never in the world, not without trucking facilities. So what was they up to? Carpet selling? When I got here, I was surprised because there was no signs, no smell of a business having been carried on. You know what I mean?'

'Not exactly,' Eric said carefully.

'There was no feel to the place. Dust, yeah, empty space. But no confidence. It was my guess there'd been no activity in the place for months before I moved in.'

Gravely Eric said, 'It's true the business that had been carried on here had got into severe financial difficulties '

Waverley made an obscene remark; the girl's head lifted, but it was as much at Eric's presence as her father's obscenity. She gave Waverley an annoyed glance, then turned back to her work. 'It wasn't very clean, here,' she remarked.

'I said. Dust. Not much else. Anyway, I don't know what all this has to do with me. I say maybe this feller skipped and you get a bit excited. It's only a guess. What do you want from me?'

'I wondered if you might be able to tell me where Crane had gone.'

'Like I said, never even met him.'

'What about Stonier?'

Waverley pursed his lips. 'Now, that's a bit different. I never met him, neither, but shortly after we got started here there was a request came in — there'd been some hitch or other in the registration of the lease and I was told we needed to get a signature from the Stonier feller. Took us a little time to find him, as I recall, because he'd left the area. They trailed him in the end, got a feeling it was down in the West Country somewhere. My solicitors will know. If you want to ask.'

'Why would Stonier have gone to the West Country?'

'Make a new start?' Waverley squinted at Eric truculently. 'How the hell do I know? You go talk to other lawyers, you're all the same, you got time to stand around talking. I got a business to run.'

'Dad—' the girl said reproachfully.

'Well, I have,' Waverley insisted.

It was clear there was little to be gained from further talk with the builder. Eric thanked him; the man turned on his heel and trudged back through the showroom door. Eric hesitated, then glanced at the girl. He could find out easily enough, but . . .

'Who were your father's solicitors?'

She smiled. 'Walker's. Up at Castle Gate.'

* * *

The junior partner was careful, but reasonably helpful. He could not go into details, of course, but he was prepared to take a look at the files, if Mr Ward was prepared to wait. Mr Ward was prepared to wait.

The information, when it came, was scanty enough. Fred Waverley had taken an assignment of the lease from Peter Stonier and Charles Crane; after completion, and when the builder was already in possession and about to carry out certain alterations to the property, there had been raised an issue regarding rights of way. It had been necessary to contact one of the assignors; they had been unable to trace Charles Crane, but had finally managed to track down Peter Stonier with the help of an inquiry agent. He had started a new business, selling cars, in Tiverton, Devon.

Eric hesitated, and the precise, pinstripe-suited solicitor facing him across the desk raised his eyebrows. 'I'm afraid there's little more assistance I can give, Mr Ward.'

'The lease . . . assigned to Fred Waverley. In whose name was the lease? I had assumed it was in the name of the company that Stonier and Crane ran on the premises.'

'Mmmm. They sold carpets, I understand,' the junior partner said, and wrinkled his nose. 'Just let me check again . . . No, here it is: the business they ran was not a limited company, but a partnership.'

'So the lease was held by them *jointly*?'

'That is correct.'

'Which means *both* partners will have signed the assignment when it was made over to Fred Waverley.'

'As a matter of law, that is perfectly correct,' the junior partner said in a faintly surprised tone.

'And that is what happened?' Eric persisted.

'What do you mean?'

'Both Charles Crane and Peter Stonier signed the assignment of the lease.'

The junior partner allowed himself a supercilious smile. 'Of course. It could not otherwise have taken effect. The later issue of the right of way, that could be dealt with by reference to Mr Stonier alone, since all that was required was an affidavit.' He steepled his fingers, stared at them with a vaguely bored air. 'But I don't see your problem. All I can do is assure you that all that was necessary to be done *was* done.'

'*Both* partners added their signatures to the deed of assignment?'

'Correct.'

There seemed little point in pursuing the matter further with the junior partner. The fact remained, nevertheless: Peter Stonier had told Sandra Crane he had no idea where her husband had gone — yet some time afterwards, both he *and* Charles Crane had put their signatures to a document concerning the business premises in York. It would seem that Peter Stonier had told Sandra Crane something less than the truth.

* * *

He had flown in on the Friday afternoon when the southern horizon had seemed to be welded against a sky of the same colour: an azure blue, over which a haze spilled like a soft, shimmering blanket. That evening he had taken a hired car for the drive to La Canebière and late at night, before he reached his hotel, he had been forced to deal with the torrent of noisy cars that poured through the narrow streets. Now, early on the Saturday morning, the sun lanced past the curtains he had forgotten to draw and as he looked out across the old town with its terracotta-coloured houses with red-tile roofs, the breeze was light and fresh. Shutters swung open as the town awoke, laundry being bustled onto sagging lines to dry in the morning air. A cart laden with wine casks trundled past his window, a dog paced across the yard to seek the first morning shade, two black cats preened themselves on the sunlit doorstep. It was a long way from Newcastle.

The appointment with Halliday Arthur Lansley had been fixed for eleven o'clock; vaguely, it had been suggested that Lansley would arrange for him to be picked up at the hotel: it seemed he had an office in Marseilles, but spent no time there at weekends. So Eric had time in hand to partake of a leisurely breakfast of hot croissants and coffee and stroll in the morning sunshine through the town itself. It had been a mediaeval settlement, and although the old settlement itself had now been submerged in the huddle of modern buildings, there was still the three-hundred-year-old fortress, the yachts lifting quietly in the slow ripple of the harbour in an explosion of colour, and a conglomeration of sail and power rimming the ancient Quayside.

The girl arrived at his hotel at precisely eleven o'clock.

She was a surprise. Her hair was long, blonde and untidy; her skin was dark and sun-tanned, her arms and shoulders bare under a ragged shirt, and the faded jeans were patched and worn, cut off below the knee. Her eyes seemed enormous, deep brown in colour, and she was no more than twenty years of age.

'Mr Ward? My name is Jeanne-Marie.' She had a surprisingly deep voice, slightly husky, and her grip was frank and strong as she shook his hand.

'You've come to collect me?'

'Mr Lansley is at the *Alouette*, the boat, down at the harbour. He asked that I bring you to him.' She smiled, proud at the control of language. 'We can go at once?'

Eric hesitated, glancing at his clothes. He wore a light jacket and casual slacks, but was hardly dressed for sailing. Jeanne-Marie interpreted his uneasiness. 'It can be provided,' she assured him, and, nodding, turned and led the way from the coolness of the hotel lobby into the hard sunshine of the street.

Eric was already familiar with the walk down to the harbour so was able to concentrate upon the girl leading him, as she walked slightly ahead of him. Her accent betrayed a careful education, and her English was good, but her connection with Lansley would, he guessed, be neither that of a secretarial or blood relationship. She moved sinuously, swinging along in shabby canvas shoes, but he knew that her casual dress was deliberate. There would be occasions when Halliday would dress her In elegant gowns, of that Eric Ward was sure.

Jeanne-Marie made no attempt to engage him in conversation as she picked her way along the Quayside, past the fishing boats and along the moorings that jutted out into the harbour like long wooden fingers, around which clustered the sleek yachts with their varied coloured pennants. The *Alouette* was at the far end of the moorings, its powerful body a gleaming white, shark-like in appearance, powerful in its promise. On the foredeck two men stood smoking, casually: they both wore jeans and maroon-coloured shirts, almost a uniform. They were uniform also in their muscularity and the sharpness of their glance: their eyes ignored Jeanne-Marie, a sign of their professionalism as far as Eric was concerned.

The girl preceded him along the gangplank; when she stepped aboard she stopped, turned, smiled at Eric and made a brief gesture towards the after cockpit, and then turned left herself, to go forward and disappear into the lounge. Eric looked about uncertainly, then proceeded towards the after cockpit.

'You like her?'

The speaker was perhaps sixty years of age, sixteen stone in weight, not more than five feet three in height. He was standing under the striped awning that had converted the after cockpit into a shadowed lounge; his belly sagged above a pair of faded denim shorts, the only clothing he wore, if one discounted the gold chain encircling his wrist. His skin was deeply tanned, but dappled in white patches that denoted a skin complaint of some kind and although he was completely bald, vigorous red, and white, hair sprouted from his chest and matted his shoulders. His eyes were small, an innocent china-blue in colour above fat, contented cheeks, and his mouth was generous and charming. There was a Pickwickian air of contentedness about him which Eric found disarming: at the same time he recollected some of the things he had heard about Halliday Arthur Lansley, and he withheld judgment: the charming mouth could, no doubt, set like a steel trap on occasions, and the innocence of the blue eyes could turn to ice.

'She's . . . very nice.'

The blue eyes flickered over him, summing him up, and the fat man smiled. 'I was talking about the *Alouette*, of course, but Jeanne-Marie, she also is quite . . . charming.'

'You're Mr. Lansley?'

'I am. And you're Mr Ward,' the fat man said with a mocking gravity. 'Would you like a drink? Some iced lemonade, or barley water?'

Eric Ward stared at him. 'You've done some homework on me, Mr Lansley.'

'*Had* it done, dear boy. Yes, I know that alcohol doesn't suit you too much since you've had trouble with glaucoma. But I know a lot more than that about you and about your reputation. Perceptive, sensitive, honest . . .' He grinned, disarmingly. 'Not exactly the usual qualities one discerns in a lawyer.'

'Why did you consider it necessary to make such inquiries?' Eric asked, somewhat nettled.

'Know your enemies, know your friends,' Lansley replied. He turned, moved along the deck, light on his feet as many heavyweight men often seemed to be, and reached into the icebox set under the bulkhead. 'Lemonade, then?'

'That'll do.'

'That's right,' Lansley said as he poured two measures of the ice-cold drink into frosted tumblers. 'As soon as the request came through from Newcastle that I speak to you, give you a statement or even an affidavit, I took the trouble to ask some friends of mine to find out about you. I still have *some* friends in the UK,' he added with a mischievous chuckle.

Eric accepted the lemonade, sipped it, and felt its iciness bring a welcome ache to his forehead. 'We're all grateful that you feel able to see me.'

'In the right surroundings, in the right surroundings,' Lansley said, waving his glass expansively. 'There's no way I'd have come back to England — and let's be clear, there's no way you'll get me to give evidence in your suit against Sheridan Enterprises.'

'We thought that an unlikely contingency.'

Lansley laughed explosively. 'I like that! In fact, a *bloody* unlikely contingency!' He settled down with a grunt into a canvas chair and waved Eric to another, set against the awning. 'No, I don't mind talking to you here, under this sky, away from all the troubles that went on back in England. But I'm sixty-three now, not as fit as I was . . . at least, for some things,' he added with a hint of a leer, 'and I've no desire to experience the cold winds of the North. You had the good sense to take rooms in the old town.'

'That's right,' Eric said, slightly taken aback at the sudden turn in the conversation.

'Sensible. What I expected. I like the Vieille Ville. It's kept its winding streets, its mediaeval stonework, its tiny shops. You can still get that elusive whiff of cooking from unseen kitchens. The Nazis called the old town a menace to health, and tried to raze it.'

'Is that so?'

'They were really concerned about *their* health: the old town was actually a centre for the Resistance. Concern for *my* health brought me out here, and I'll not go back, except maybe in a pine box. But I still like to moor here in the evenings, see the old men putting in their trawlers at the harbour in La Canebière, see the fishwives putting out the fish for sale in the mornings. I'm sentimental, you see.'

Eric didn't believe it, but said nothing.

'It's why I'm prepared to see you, talk to you,' Lansley went on. 'Echoes of Northumberland. Lovely country.'

The sudden, subdued rumble and thunder of the engines startled Eric. White water boiled at the stern as one of the two maroon-shirted men leaped ashore to cast off the mooring lines. 'What's happening?' he asked.

'Twin Mercury outboards, powerful enough to keep me ahead of the mistral when it funnels down the Rhone Valley and spills into the Golfe du Lion.'

'Mr Lansley—'

'Relax, my friend. Why should we sit in some stuffy office in Marseilles and talk when we can be out at sea, enjoying life as it is meant to be enjoyed? You are aboard the *Alouette* — enjoy her. We'll talk in a little while, after lunch maybe. Meanwhile, in the small cabin you'll find some suitable clothing. Why not change, and settle down with the sun and sea?'

The cabin was small but airy; through the bulkhead he could hear the sound of movement in the galley, but in the hanging locker he found a light sports shirt and shorts and swimsuit. The folding table, he discovered on investigation, served not only as a dining table and desk top but also converted into a comfortable berth. When he came back on deck and made his way to the after cockpit, the *Alouette* was surging serenely across a mirrored blue sea and Halliday Arthur Lansley was now accompanied by three young women. Gravely, but with mischievous eyes, he introduced them: 'Villette, Catherine, and of course you've already met Jeanne-Marie.'

They were stereotypes: each blonde, dark-eyed, lissom-figured, and wearing as little as possible. They were not ostentatious, however: Lansley clearly liked elements of control in his girls.

They were good conversationalists, nevertheless, and Lansley relaxed as the five of them sat under the awning, enjoying the cool breeze in the heat of the day and the *Alouette* surged past a seacoast that consisted of towering limestone cliffs, bleak and treeless as Norway's North Cape. The talk was light and inconsequential with Lansley presiding over it all like a paternalistic, considerate uncle, except for the occasional caress of a tanned shoulder, or the odd gleam as he watched Jeanne-Marie or the equally blonde Catherine. The man who had cast off came to the cockpit shortly with some cheese, crusty bread, fruit and rose wine from Provence. In the afternoon the *Alouette* turned past a headland clustered with pastel-roofed houses and a green fan of vineyards, and slipped into one of the numerous *calanques,* a drowned valley formed by long vanished streams. Eric swam with Catherine in the cold, clear water, and her body was a slim, lithe, twisting thing in the green underwater twilight.

In the late afternoon, with a bottle of Chablis before him, Lansley at last seemed inclined to talk of the matters that had brought Eric Ward to him. 'So what exactly is it that you want from me, Mr Ward?'

'Background information, really — and certain confirmations.'

'Regarding Sheridan Enterprises, and my dealings with them.' The owner of the *Alouette* pursed his lips thoughtfully. 'Well, yes, I think I can do this for you. Where do you want me to start?'

'The beginning?'

'A good place,' Lansley said, smiling, 'but too far back. Let's just take that unhappy period of my life when I became . . . shall we say . . . overstretched?'

'Was that before or after you started your dealing with Morcomb Estates?' Eric asked.

'Well, let's put it like this. The signs were there that the sharks were sharpening their teeth, but I had every confidence that I could outswim them. The dealings with Morcomb Estates, believe me, they were undertaken in all good faith. The countryside of Northumberland is unsurpassable for rough shooting — but I don't need to tell you that. I had negotiated with Morcomb Estates for a considerable tract of land: the contacts I had made in Saudi made me confident that I could put together a package deal which would bring those flowing-robed gentlemen across to Northumberland in considerable numbers. Even Saudis,' he added drily, 'will go for a package deal, if it's *expensive* enough.'

'It never came off.'

Lansley scratched at a white patch of skin on his arm thoughtfully. 'I was . . . unlucky. I had a cash flow problem at that time, and I was also dependent for certain finance on business acquaintances in the Middle East. About that time, you'll recall, everything went more than a little haywire. The Shah lost his Peacock Throne, all hell boiled up in Iran — well, let's just say that it was the wrong time, as far as I was concerned, for the Inland Revenue to start pressing buttons they'd conveniently ignored for years.'

'So cash flow problems caused your withdrawal from the Northumberland deals?'

'That's it. Morcomb Estates were sensible: if they'd pressed me really hard they'd have blown the lot and got virtually nothing in the pound. Instead, we compromised.'

'El Centro.'

'Correct.' Lansley sipped at his drink and glanced around at the dark sea. 'The Mexico deal was a sound one, but, well, it was just too early for me. The Inland Revenue were on my back, I was in trouble with Morcomb Estates, so I had to cut back on my futures. I gave your solicitors the details: they had the chance to go into it carefully. The upshot of it all was that they accepted a transfer of my shares in the El Centro deal as the price of my withdrawal from the Northumberland contract.'

'I'm not sure they were wise.'

Lansley chuckled. 'Hindsight, boy, hindsight. All I can really tell you is that it was clean when I made the transfer; whatever Sheridan Enterprises are up to now, it's nothing to do with me.'

Eric hesitated. 'There seems to be some . . . confusion about who owns Sheridan.'

'It sure as hell isn't me,' Lansley said.

'And you have no interest in the company?'

Lansley watched him for a few moments, amusement registered in his little eyes. '*Interest.* By that you mean a legal interest, I guess, rather than just curiosity. Look, Ward, I like you. If I've got an *interest* in Sheridan, it's an insignificant one, and unlikely to upturn any Morcomb apple carts.'

'But if you are a shareholder, and any hint of collusion appears in the legality of the transfer being questioned, the fact that you hold an interest at all could raise issues of fraud.'

'Fraud?' Lansley chuckled again. 'You think I'm fool enough to get caught twice? I know all about fraud. When the Inland Revenue stripped me, or *tried* to strip me before throwing me inside for a couple of years, I learned all about fraud — I had the legal jargon coming out of my ears. But the fact is they couldn't nail me hard then, and they can't do it now. I served my time — albeit shortened by a heart attack that persuaded them I ought to be released on humanitarian grounds — and I came out clean.'

Eric glanced around him, at the yacht and the cliffs some half-mile distant. 'There are some who feel you came out more than simply . . . clean.'

Lansley waved his glass in an expansive gesture. 'A man in his sixties has earned the right to enjoy a few of the comforts. The Government seemed not disposed to strip me of everything. But then, there were people in *relatively* high places who owed me something. Those days are, alas, now gone.'

'You will not, as you say, come back to England to give evidence—'

'My state of health, Mr Ward, forbids such exercise or anxiety,' Lansley said smoothly.

'But are you prepared to make the necessary affidavits that we might use in the suit?'

'My dear boy, you dictate them if you wish and I'll sign them. After you've seen the papers and ascertained their legality, of course . . .'

* * *

Lansley could not have been more helpful. Eric spent the rest of the day, until the light began to fail, sitting in the after cockpit reading and checking the documentation that Lansley provided from the heavy briefcase he brought up on deck. The man himself disappeared below, perhaps for a siesta or possibly something more vigorous, and Eric was happy enough to spend the time dealing with the papers. He drafted some notes, annotated in pencil a few of the documents with queries he would need to raise with Lansley and later, back home, and started a draft of a statement he wanted from Lansley himself. The sun settled like a great orange globe into the darkening horizon and there was the sound of movement forward. Eric packed the papers away as he heard someone come to the after cockpit. It was Catherine, her long blonde hair carefully brushed, elegant in a white sheath dress that set off her tanned skin to perfection.

'Mr Lansley will be expecting you in twenty minutes, for dinner,' she said.

An hour later, with several martinis inside a voluble Lansley, and with the three girls seated with them, Eric sat down in the small dining-room of the *Alouette*. It was a convivial meal; the girls chattered in lively fashion, Catherine paid Eric considerable attention, and Lansley, in white jacket and bow tie, was in high good spirits.

'Ah, Mr Ward, these you must savour — the *violets des roches*. You have not tasted them? Ah, the first time, it is like this.' He grimaced, pursing his lips, emphasizing the taste. 'Later, you come to like them; washed down with white wine they are magnificent. Besides—' he smiled at Jeanne-Marie as he caressed her brown shoulder — 'there are other reasons.'

'How do you mean?' Eric asked, aware as he did so he was being led innocently to a trap.

'Because they contain the vital elements of the sea,' the older man laughed, 'and you become younger by ten years if you eat them! Ask Jeanne-Marie here — she will tell you I need the years!'

Eric was not impressed. He tried the dish: they tasted like rubber tyres soaked in fish oil. With a dash of iodine. Lansley enjoyed the grimace he was unable to control.

Later, it proved impossible to bring the conversation back to business. The *Alouette* slipped into a harbour that lay like a pool of mercury under the moon. Beyond a palm-girt rind of sand lazy threads of smoke rose from the tiny fishing village set against a steep hillside that merged with the dark blue sky. From somewhere on the hill Eric could hear the trills and arpeggios of a nightingale, its song as ethereal as the moonlight itself. And Lansley was expansive.

'Ah, rocks red as rust, turquoise coves, pines green as spring, the woods of cork oaks . . . do you understand why I would never wish to return, Mr Ward? And who knows, in another few decades much of what is simple here might be gone. Lord Brougham has much to answer for. Cholera forced him to winter in this area in eighteen thirty-four. He liked it so much he came back for the next thirty-four years. And popularized the area with the English.'

The brandy had obviously warmed him, and he had become more obvious in his attentions to the cool Jeanne-Marie. The other two girls had fallen silent, sipping their brandy and enjoying the warm night air and the rhythm of the lifting yacht as it rode at anchor. It was midnight before Eric, who felt relaxed and at ease, finally announced his retirement. Lansley waved a negligent left hand; his right was busy with Jeanne-Marie.

In his cabin, the air was warm and close. Desultory drifts of conversation came down to him from the dining area; at one point there was the sound of breaking glass. Eric undressed and lay naked on top of the sheets of his bunk, and in a little while as the night breeze lifted he felt cool air touch his skin, and he drifted off to sleep.

He awoke with a start some time later, not certain what had disturbed him. He lay there for a moment, puzzled, his pulse racing as he tried to focus his mind and his eyes to the unfamiliar surroundings. Then he became aware there was a woman standing at the side of his bunk.

The long blonde hair drifted about her shoulders; she stood quite still and as he stared at her he could make out the tiny white triangle that was her briefs. It was all she wore; the diffused moonlight touched the curve of her breasts, darkly shadowing them, outlining the line of her hip and thigh. She leaned forward. 'Mr Ward.'

It was Catherine. He remembered the shape of her in the green water and his body moved.

'I thought you might be lonely.'

She put out a hand and touched him lightly; her fingers were cool and supple.

'Was this Lansley's idea?'

'Mine. But what difference does it make?'

'He might be displeased, if he knew you were here.'

'He would not. He is with Jeanne-Marie.' Her face was near his now, her mouth approaching his and he was aware of the soft curves of her body, the faint hint of perfume in his nostrils. Her hands moved swiftly over him, expertly, and he trembled, then caught at her wrist.

'You do not like this?'

'Now wait a minute.'

'I can please. There are other ways.'

'I think you should stop,' Eric said thickly.

'The way you looked at me this afternoon,' she said quietly. 'I knew what was in your mind.'

'No,' Eric said, and sat up, held her by the shoulders.

'I do not understand,' she murmured.

'Neither do I. But I don't think you should stay here.' She stood there for a little while, looking down at him, cool, controlled and professional. He thought, in the darkness, that she was smiling. She put out a hand again, caressed him, and she knew.

'The night will be long,' she said.

'I've no doubt,' he replied.

She left then, and the night was long.

* * *

The *Alouette* slipped out of harbour in the early dawn, when Eric had fallen into a disturbed, fitful sleep in which

Anne was with him in some deep, green cavern full of shimmering, drifting lights. When he finally woke he lay in his bunk for a while, listening to the rushing sound of the water, and wondering about the evening and the night and Lansley. At last he dressed and went out to the after cockpit.

Halliday Arthur Lansley was already there, talking to one of the maroon-jerseyed crewmen. There was no sign of the girls, and Lansley was dressed in a sweater that seemed to emphasize his bulk, canvas trousers and rope soled sandals. As Eric came forward the crewman was dismissed and Lansley looked at Eric, smiling lopsidedly. 'Good morning,' he said.

'Good morning.' Eric looked about him. To the north was a long, brooding headland behind which dark clouds seemed to boil against the bright sunshine. The wind was cold and he shivered suddenly.

Catching his glance, Lansley explained, 'North-west gale coming up. The waves will be heaping soon; it's the mistral, and time we went back to La Canebière. Did you . . . er . . . sleep well?'

Eric looked at him carefully. 'It *was* your idea, then.'

'Seemed the courteous thing to do,' Lansley said affably.

'But unnecessary. As unnecessary as the rest of it.'

Lansley's face was suddenly still, and the innocence had vanished from his blue eyes. Uncertainty touched his mouth, bruising it and wiping away its friendliness. 'I'm not quite certain what you mean.'

'You're certain, all right. And deliberate. I'm just not clear why.'

'You'll have to explain yourself, Mr Ward.'

Eric grinned, shook his head. 'Oh, I've enjoyed it, the treatment. We could have done all that was necessary in a few hours in your office, but I've appreciated the trip, the swimming, the food . . . and the company, even if I did feel it necessary to reject part of it last night.'

'Why *did* you reject it, Mr Ward?'

'There are a number of reasons,' Eric said levelly. 'But just one will do. I don't want to feel that I owe anyone anything, particularly when I don't know when the debt will be called in.'

'That was a mere gift last night,' Lansley said.

'No. You don't make gifts. You're not that sort of man.'

'What kind of man am I, then?'

'The sort who would not agree to help Morcomb Estates for nothing; who would not bother to show me such hospitality; who would not go so far as to offer me a woman. Not unless it was all to be some part of a bargain. The question is — what is there that I, or Morcomb Estates, can offer you?'

Lansley laughed, but there was a brittleness to the sound. 'You're a direct man, Ward, but I appreciate that. I don't know that I can *react* to it—'

'You have to. Or you don't get what you want.' Lansley stared at him for a few moments, then turned, dropped his bulk into a canvas chair and glanced towards the brooding headland to the north. 'I still have friends in the north of England, but not many. I thought you might be . . . recruited.'

'What the hell is that supposed to mean?' Eric asked.

'Recruitment is a crude word. Look, Mr Ward, I admit I have been . . . cultivating you these last two days. You ask why. The answer is simple enough. From Morcomb Estates I expect nothing, and it had not been my intention to help them in any degree. But then I was told you were being briefed to act for them, and I made some local inquiries, and I liked what I heard. So I decided I wanted to meet you, talk to you.'

'With what purpose in mind?'

'I understand you have more than a merely professional interest in Morcomb Estates.'

'Mr Lansley,' Eric said coldly, 'I ought to make some thing clear. I don't mix matrimony with business.'

'But you are nevertheless *interested* in the affairs of the company,' Lansley insisted. 'All right. I tell you, I have showed you the supporting documentation, I have proved title, and I am prepared to make supporting affidavits. That will help your wife's company.'

'And in return?'

'Ah, well . . .' Lansley was silent for a little while, his eyes lidded, his hands quiescent over his paunch. 'I've no intention of returning to England. I still have some friends there. I also have other . . . acquaintances. Men whose whereabouts and activities I would welcome news of, from time to time.'

'Is that where I come in?'

'Precisely.'

'An inquiry agent—'

Lansley held up a plump hand. 'I do not like inquiry agents. They are untrustworthy. They change sides. Lawyers do not. And I hear you *are* trustworthy — indeed, endowed with a certain strict honesty and code of ethics, I understand. Strange, for a lawyer.' He chuckled, heaved himself forward in his seat and groped in the back pocket of his trousers for a wallet. From the leather wallet he withdrew a photograph, and stared at it for a little while. Then he passed it to Eric.

It was a snapshot of a man standing on a wharf. He wore rough seaman's clothing, his hair was cut *en brosse*, and his narrow face had a lean sharpness about it that suggested a cold intensity. There was something familiar about the background of cranes.

'North Shields,' Lansley said quietly. 'A photograph taken fairly recently. His name is Bartlett — Donald Bartlett.'

'Who is he?'

'Let us say . . . an acquaintance. Have you ever seen him?'

'Not to my knowledge.'

Lansley was watching Eric carefully. 'You're certain of that?'

Wordlessly, Eric handed the photograph back. Lansley accepted it with a degree of reluctance, staring at it again briefly, before committing it back to the wallet. 'All I want you to do, Mr Ward, is to inform me if you see this man in your . . . peregrinations around Tyneside. It would also be helpful to me if you were to tell me what you think he might be doing.'

'You said you had friends in the North. Why can't they do it?'

'They are afraid, Mr Ward.'

The menace that hung behind the words seemed to infect the after cockpit. Eric waited, but Lansley said no more for a little while, seemingly sunk in contemplation of the deck. At last, Eric said, 'I suppose this is in some way tied up with your operations in the narcotics market.'

Lansley's head snapped up, in spite of himself. His mouth opened as though he were about to speak, but he restrained himself with an effort, and when he did speak his tone was level and controlled. 'That is an interesting observation, Mr Ward. I cannot imagine what prompted it.'

'Something you said, something I'd heard. Drugs have been a larger problem on Tyneside for the last few years than people are prepared to admit. There is a rumour you were deeply involved in the business, trundling shipments over into Teesside, Manchester and maybe elsewhere. The rumour adds that the fraud charges against you could have been much worse, except that you cooperated with the police, allowed your own links to be destroyed with the smugglers in exchange for . . . leniency?'

'An interesting thesis, Mr Ward. Please go on.'

'You told me yesterday that you had a cash flow problem. It arose when the Shah fell. That's when the hatches were battened down on the normal supply runs. If you were deeply committed financially to cargoes of narcotics, maybe that's why you had a cash flow problem — and had to do a deal as well. And if you *did* do a deal, maybe some . . . *acquaintances* got hurt. Was this man Bartlett one of them?'

Some of the tension had gone from Lansley's body, but he was still careful, his voice tight. 'Fanciful, Mr Ward, but interesting. I won't deny I haven't been involved in certain smuggling activities from time to time. Indeed, there were exciting times in the late 'sixties, when I ran some very profitable cargo — Pakistanis who were eager to evade our immigration laws. They used to congregate in Amsterdam, and I used to get them ashore on the Cleveland coast, at Robin Hood's Bay. Romantic, don't you think? Lorries then, to Leeds. Profitable . . . and exciting. But drugs?' He looked at Eric lazily. 'You can hardly expect me to make such a damaging admission.'

'Nevertheless, you want this man Bartlett traced.'

'I didn't say *traced*. *No*, nothing so formal. I wish to put you to no such trouble, Mr Ward. I will help Morcomb Estates. In return, you will tell me if you ever see Don Bartlett on Tyneside. And if you *happen* to discover what he's up to, and why, I'd be grateful for the information. *Early*.'

'It seems a small enough task,' Eric said warily.

'Very small.'

As the *Alouette* fled before the dark clouds to the harbour of La Canebière, Lansley was as good as his word, and completed the affidavits that would be helpful to Morcomb Estates in their action against Sheridan Enterprises, Inc. Eric mulled over what he had been told and concluded there was little harm in complying with Lansley's request — particularly since he suspected he would never be in a position to give the man the assistance he really needed. The chance of crossing Bartlett's path, if he were on Tyneside, must surely be slim.

'Do you always get what you want, Lansley?'

'Not always. Or otherwise why would I be here?'

'My wife has followed your career. She thinks you're the kind who could get away with murder.'

The coldness of Lansley's blue eyes belied the easy charm of his smile. 'Your wife,' he said, '*might* be described as a most perceptive woman. But then, what woman is not?'

CHAPTER 3

1

The man in the dock was of middle height, burly, and wore the dark blue suit with an air of discomfort. The hands that gripped the rail in front of him were coarse-haired; the whiteness of the knuckles betrayed a nervousness that was not shown in his face as he glared truculently at Eric Ward. From his seat, Eddie Stevens watched and listened as the solicitor began his questioning of the man who had beaten Eddie Stevens above Rothbury Crags.

'Your name is Frank Penry?'

'Already said so.'

'You are the owner of the dog that was used to bait the badger on the hill, I understand.'

'Working,' Penry said with a scowl. 'He was *working* the badger.'

'The intention either way,' Ward said quietly, 'was, presumably, to kill the animal.'

Penry shook his head decisively. 'You got it wrong. We don't go out to kill the buggers. It's not like that bloodthirsty fox-huntin' lot. This is *real* sport. We set the dogs on, reach the badger, but all we do after that is pull them out, smack their arses and send them on their way.'

'It seems a bit pointless, Mr Penry.'

'It's sport. Thrill of the hunt, you can call it.'

'And not cruel?' Ward asked.

Penry hesitated, then scratched his cheek thoughtfully. His glance strayed towards Eddie Stevens, watching impassively from the well of the magistrates' courtroom. 'Cruel? They gas badgers, you know, some of the farmers. That's worse than what we do. With gas, a badger can have a slow death underground.'

'Whereas all you do,' Ward suggested smoothly, 'is . . . "smack their arses," I think you said. And there's no cruelty?'

Frank Penry hesitated again, glanced towards the magistrate and shook his head. 'Be daft, wouldn't I, to say there was *no* cruelty. There's a bit, aye, but the main pain is to the dogs.'

The magistrate raised his head and looked at Eric Ward. 'I've no doubt, Mr Ward, that all this is most interesting and would be relevant if we were dealing with the matter of a prosecution under the Wild Life and Countryside Act, but you are acting on the instructions of Mr. Stevens to deal with a matter of common assault and battery, are you not?'

'That is so, but if you will permit me—'

'A little more licence, Mr Ward, but only a little more, unless you return soon to the matters in hand.'

Silly old sod, Eddie Stevens said to himself under his breath. Hadn't he seen the photographs Eddie had already published in the Sundays?

'The main pain is to the dogs,' Ward continued. 'I understand your own dog was torn rather badly on the side, and the second animal was injured on the muzzle.'

'That silly bitch was supposed to stand off and bark. Nothing more. Served her right, getting stuck in when we hauled the old badger out.'

'And your own dog?'

'Look,' Penry said forcefully, 'the dogs love it. If they didn't, they'd never go down into those tunnels, not after the first time and an early mauling. All right, if you want to know how it is, I've lost three dogs over the years with suffocation in the tunnels. They get stuck down there, or the old badger pulls them in and buries them with soil. As a matter of fact there was one point that night when I thought I'd lost my dog, but he came through all right.'

'Burial,' Ward said drily, 'would seem to be an occupational hazard, then, for your dogs?'

'They *enjoy* the hunt,' Penry said defensively.

'You always let the badger go?'

'Yes.'

'I would like to read out to you a newspaper cutting from the *Journal*, two years ago. *We killed one in a sett up near Make-me-Rich last week. Hell of a fight it gave. Its nose and lips got torn right back to the rear of its skull and one of its legs was snapped in half and hanging by the joint. Its sides were just chewed to pieces.* Have you ever been on such a hunt?'

'That was nothing to do with me.'

'You work the area above Ponteland?'

'Sometimes.'

'But this quotation wasn't given by one of your group?'

'I don't know about that.'

'One of the men out with you the night the assault on Mr Stevens took place was Ian Timothy,' Ward said quietly. 'He is quoted in this newspaper report. On that occasion he was fined seventy pounds.'

'I wasn't there.'

'But if you had been, *would you have been concerned*?'

Truculently, his cheeks beginning to redden, Penry said in a harsh tone, 'It's *sport*, and not nothing different from wearing a red coat and riding about with a whip and a posh accent and getting away with tearing foxes to bits! Look, a badger can take a lot of pain, and give it. I've seen one run across a field with a Jack Russell terrier in its teeth. I've never been one to bring in the lurchers which can roll a badger over and hold its head so it can't bite and the smaller dogs can get in. And I've seen men match a badger in a trench against a Staffordshire bull terrier, and all right, I've killed a badger myself, with an iron bar, but the *real* sport is not to kill, it's to find the sow, dig her out, and then let her go.'

'And the blood, and the pain, and the terror are merely incidentals?' Ward asked.

'They're all part of the game, damn it!'

'And because you're used to blood and pain, and see it as just part of the game, is that why you felt no compunction about almost beating Mr Stevens to death?' The courtroom was silent. The magistrate waited, watching Penry carefully as the man glared at Eric Ward, angry, resentful. 'I didn't say I *did* beat him.'

'But you were up there that night,' Ward insisted, 'for the photographs that were taken prove it. And you were expecting blood and pain and excitement, and suddenly much of the excitement was taken away from you. And that's why you went after him; your blood lust was up—'

'I was just trying to get the film back,' Penry interrupted.

'But the photographer had already escaped with the film when you reached Stevens. You could have backed off then, but you wanted blood and pain, you wanted violence and excitement, and, resentful because you'd lost the fun of allowing your dogs to bite a badger to death, you took it into your head to seek revenge on the journalist who had surprised you!'

'He had a go at me—'

'He'd run for a mile! He was breathless, exhausted, scared. There were four of you — and you suggest *he* attacked *you*?'

Penry was silent for a few moments, but his jaw was set hard and a wild light shone in his eyes as pent-up resentments struggled to the surface. 'You . . . all this, it makes me sick! What's wrong with a bit of fun at night? The badgers, the dogs . . . ah, the hell with it. What right did that bastard have to interfere? I don't bother him — why should he stick his newspaper nose into my business,? He got what he deserved, a bloody good hiding, and—'

'And you'd do the same again, in similar circumstances?' Eric Ward asked quietly.

Frank Penry stood staring at him, furiously, but made no further reply.

* * *

Later, in the sunshine outside the magistrates' court, Eddie Stevens thanked Eric Ward. 'You set him up pretty well,' he said.

'There was little doubt of a conviction,' Ward replied. 'I merely wanted to make sure the sentence was sufficient. Penry is a dangerous man and a brutal one.'

'I've got bruises enough to prove it,' Stevens announced feelingly. 'Yeah, you did a good job, even though I think you went a bit overboard saying I was breathless, exhausted and scared.'

'Weren't you?' Eric asked, grinning.

'You wouldn't believe!' Stevens shook his head. 'No, I'm glad Penry copped it: that lad's as dangerous as a cat with the clap, and as mean. We're safer with him cooling off inside for a bit. Now then, can I give you a lift?'

Eric explained he had finished for the day and would be meeting his wife Anne at the flat in Gosforth before they returned together to the house in Northumberland. The journalist clapped him on the shoulder. 'No problem. I'm going up to Gosforth myself, to call in at the pathology laboratories to see how they're getting on. I feel I have a kind of proprietary interest in what they're holding there — you know, the corpse I found up at Rothbury Crags? I need to keep abreast of it as a story, of course, but there's also the feeling he's kind of . . . mine, you know?'

Eric accepted the offer of a lift since he was aware there was likely to be a dearth of taxis available anywhere other than near Central Station, and when Stevens suggested they call at the forensic laboratories first and for Eric to come in with him, he agreed readily enough since he was forced to admit to a degree of curiosity himself about the find Stevens had made on the Crags.

The police officer in charge of liaison with the staff at the laboratories was well known to Stevens and Eric himself had come across him from time to time. After a brief chat with him, Stevens led the way to the office of Dr Summers, a small, white-haired, bow-tied individual in a white coat whose office looked as though a violent gust of wind had rearranged his filing for him. There were papers everywhere, and books stacked untidily on the shelves, files perched in unsteady piles on the floor, threatening drunkenly to slide into a heap in the corner. Dr Summers wiped his hand on the backside of his trousers before shaking hands with Eric. 'Pleased to meet you.'

'You don't exactly inspire confidence in the efficacy of our forensic service in Newcastle,' Stevens admonished, gazing around him.

'What's important is up here,' Dr Summers said, tapping his left temple with an air of faded, weary wisdom, 'and not to be trepanned out by the likes of you.'

'Now you know I've always cooperated,' Stevens said. 'The odd bottle of Glenfiddich, yes.'

'And I've never *pried*.'

'Not more'n most,' Dr Summers admitted, and shuffled behind his cluttered desk. 'But what are you in here for now? Your favourite felony?'

'It *was* murder, then?'

'He hardly tapped himself on the head and then buried himself at Rothbury Crags,' the pathologist scoffed. 'Where's your investigative instincts?'

'Beaten out of me by one Frank Penry, maybe,' Stevens said with a grimace. 'Mr Ward here, he got him put away for a year, this afternoon.'

'Nice.' Dr Summers stared sourly at Eric Ward for several seconds. 'Police I can take; journalists I suffer;

cadavers I almost enjoy. Never quite categorized a lawyer. Don't care for them.'

'Oh, come on,' Stevens said with a grin. 'There's lawyers and lawyers.'

'No,' Summers said, and sniffed. 'There's just lawyers.'

Eddie Stevens broke the short silence. 'So tell me about my favourite corpse.'

'Not much to tell, really. We've worked him over now, pretty thoroughly. This isn't for printing, by the way. Off the record, or the liaison superintendent will screw me.'

'Agreed.'

'Well, far as we can tell he was about forty or so when he copped it. Death was probably caused by a blow to the head — pretty thin skull, actually. From the state of re arrangement his face seemed to have gone through I guess he was beaten about the head, although there's a little doubt.'

'Why?'

'There'd been rocks placed on him; bit of pressure. Not too likely, but they did move in heavy rains, and then erosion exposed him. Though, funnily enough, it was a pretty amateurish job.'

'What was?'

'The interment. The chap who buried him, he was certainly no member of the Gravediggers' Union. If it wasn't a stupid suggestion, I'd even testify that he was buried so's he'd be found.'

'You'd actually testify to that?'

'That's a stupid suggestion.'

Eric Ward smiled, aware that the pathologist was baiting the journalist. 'Was there anything on the body to suggest who he was?'

Dr Summers turned and inspected Eric as though surprised he could actually talk. 'Nothing. Which does away with the theory that he was *supposed* to have been found. I mean, why place a corpse in such a way that he'll turn up again in a while, and then remove rings, watch, clothing labels, papers, documents — anything that might be used to identify him? No, I guess the burial was bungled, or maybe the gravedigger was surprised, frightened off before he could do an efficient job. All I can say is that our corpse was fortyish, good teeth, about five-nine in height, pretty healthy until he got clobbered, clean shaven, and fair-haired. And he was laid to rest around about the autumn of nineteen eighty.' As an after thought, he added, 'We're sending information about his teeth around, of course, but it's a long shot. He had cavities.'

'So?'

'So he hadn't been to a dentist in maybe two years. Now look, gentlemen, I've got some filing to do, you know? I mean, had you brought a bottle with you, Stevens, maybe we could have talked longer, but in the circumstances . . .'

* * *

Eddie Stevens drove the short distance from the forensic laboratories to the Gosforth flat in silence, but when Eric made to leave the car the journalist stopped him, and cut the car engine. 'I'm grateful for your putting Penry away, like I said. I wouldn't want to be laid into like that again. But you'll recall our conversation in hospital?'

'Well enough.'

'I just wondered whether you'd managed to come up with anything that might be of interest to me.'

'I'm afraid not.'

'Lawyers reticence, or truth?' Stevens asked quizzically.

'I explained to you before—'

'Okay, okay,' Stevens soothed. 'Like I said, I'm just really asking for a kind of confirmation, a hardening up of possible leads regarding Halliday Arthur Lansley. It was never my intention to get you involved in any breach of trust as far as your clients are concerned.'

'Lansley isn't my client.'

'No, but I guess he'll have offered you some kind of deal.'

Eric turned to stare at the reporter. 'What do you mean?'

Stevens grinned and shook his head in mock amazement. 'You're not going to tell me Lansley has become philanthropic and law-abiding in his old age. He won't want to come to England, and you can't make him, just to give evidence in a civil suit, but he's prepared to talk to you in France? Come on, I didn't say it before because I was curious about what it might be, but there's surely some kind of deal between you two!'

'I don't think—'

'Don't get stuffy with me, Mr Ward! He denied the story that he might have been involved in drug smuggling, right?'

'I didn't exactly discuss it—'

'But you raised it,' Stevens interposed happily. 'I had an idea you would, if I mentioned it to you. So you raised it, he denied it. Right?'

Reluctantly Eric nodded. 'But I didn't press the issue.'

'Wouldn't have expected you to. But he did talk to you, and give you some assistance over the Morcomb suit. And he didn't throw you out when you *raised* the drug scene with him. So, what was it he was after? What was the deal?'

Stevens was fishing, Eric knew. His view of the character of Halliday Arthur Lansley was probably a correct one, but he could not *know* that Eric had no legal armlock on Lansley that would have forced the man to render assistance to the Morcomb side. Nor could he know there really had been something Lansley wanted in return. Eric had no intention of giving the reporter details of the lengths to which Lansley had been prepared to go to obtain Eric's assistance, but on the other hand Lansley was not Eric's client; he had no intention of maintaining the contact or actively promoting Lansley's interests personally, but there could be no harm in whetting Stevens's appetite and, indeed, letting him do the work Lansley had asked Eric to do.

'So what was the deal?' Stevens persisted.

Eric hesitated. 'Have you ever heard of a man called Donald Bartlett?'

'Can't say that I have,' Stevens replied immediately, and then paused. 'Now wait a minute . . . Bartlett . . . give me a clue.'

'No clue, other than that he's been tied in with our friend Lansley in the past.'

Stevens stared at Eric. 'You putting me on to something?'

'I merely asked you a question.'

'You *are* putting me on to something,' Stevens said with conviction. 'All right, I'll play along with the tight-lipped bit. Donald Bartlett . . . right, I'll make some inquiries. You'll want to know the result, of course.'

'I'm not particularly curious,' Eric replied.

'I don't understand. You want to know what I find, or not?'

'Let's say I might be interested, if it's . . . pertinent to my dealings with Lansley, and Morcomb Estates. If it's of more concern to you and your own investigations, I'm really not—'

'Hell, you really are playing it cool, aren't you?' Stevens said, and chuckled. 'All right, I can play it your way. You don't want to know unless it's something you want to know. All the ends against the middle, right? Now I know why Doc Summers don't like lawyers. He just don't understand them.'

'Don't read more into this than is really there,' Eric warned. 'You asked me to pick up any information I could that *might* be useful. The name I've given you—'

'Bartlett . . . It does tinkle some kind of small bell. I'll look into it, expecting no miracles. And I won't ask how you came by the name. All might yet be revealed, though, hey, like the bishop said to the actress!'

* * *

When he entered the flat, Eric realized that Anne had not yet returned from the meeting she had been holding with her fellow directors in Newcastle. She had told him the agenda was likely to be a long and difficult one, but that she would be back in good time so there would be no need to stay at the flat. Eric poured himself a glass of orange juice and stood by the window, staring out over the city.

He felt vaguely on edge, his nerves stretched, his pulse fluttering in a way it had used to when he was facing an attack of glaucoma. Yet the tell-tale tingling, the sharp scratching at the back of his eyes was missing: he was not due to have another bout of pain. Rather, he was aware of a sense of uneasiness, the cause of which he could not reach. It had nothing to do with his conversation with Stevens: Eric was vaguely dissatisfied with himself over that, because he had really been playing with Stevens, indulging him in a way that was unnecessary, if not unprofessional. Nor had it anything to do with his visit to La Canebière. He had not given the details of the encounter to Anne; there had been no need to do so because nothing had happened that might have caused him to feel guilty.

It had to do with Sandra. Since she had first come to see him in his office he had been aware of her presence in the background of his life. It was not that old excitements had resurfaced: their love-affair had been over long ago, killed on the day he had found her with her lover. Rather, in some vague, dissatisfying way he found himself saddled with the feeling that he owed her something. He had failed her in the days of their marriage, and indirectly she was giving him the chance to make up for it now. Yet he was reluctant to do so. Not because of Anne's opposition to his getting involved, but because he himself felt he wanted no close contact with her life, the existence she had followed when they had split up twenty years ago.

He was ashamed of that reluctance, because he would never rid himself of the feeling that he *had* failed her.

In a little while he picked up the phone. Sandra had given him a telephone number; he checked it in his pocket book and then rang the exchange.

'Sandra? It's Eric.'

'I wondered when you would ring.' She seemed tense, a slight nervousness tainting her voice. 'Have you managed to . . . find out anything?'

'I'm sorry. I've been away on business for a few days, and in court today. I've not really had time to do much as far as you're concerned. But I do have some information.'

He could understand the silence that followed, the palpable tension that was transmitted blindly over the phone to him. She wanted him to find Charles Crane; equally, there would be something inside her that wanted him *not* to find the man. 'It's . . . Charles?' she asked.

'No, nothing as dramatic as that. I've managed to trace his partner, Peter Stonier. He's got a business in Tiverton. I think I should go down to see him.'

'Yes.'

'I simply thought I should let you know . . . tell you that I'm active in the matter.'

'I see.' The tension was gone; there was a hint of relief in her voice as though she was pleased he was active, and prepared to help her, but Eric was suddenly aware of how far apart they now were. He did not know Sandra Crane, could not know her as he had known Sandra Ward. It was as well to remember that.

'I think I'd like to come down with you,' she said suddenly.

'I don't think that's necessary.'

'I'd like to.'

'It's possibly not even wise.'

'I knew Peter. He was kind to me when Charles disappeared. He might even have . . . fancied me, then, only he wasn't bold enough to . . . If I come, maybe he'd be more receptive, more helpful.'

'I'm not sure.'

'It can do no *harm*, Eric.'

He put the phone down on its receiver just as he heard Anne step into the hall.

2

Central Station was crowded. The stonework of the vast Victorian edifice had been recently cleaned and restored so that taxis and cars and buses could busily go about their pollution of the warm sandstone from scratch once again, but the crowds that thronged the echoing hall were heedless. The morning trains that pushed out towards Carlisle and York, London and Edinburgh brought in much of the bustle, but the early local commuters also thronged the station in their need to get to work on time. The morning train to Plymouth would be crowded with holidaymakers travelling midweek.

It would have been easier to fly to Bristol, and then hire a car from there to make the trip to Tiverton. But Eric's last experience of a flight had been enough to make him wary; it was true he had taken the London flight shortly after the operation for glaucoma, but he was now reluctant to repeat the experience. So it meant the Plymouth train, change at Exeter and a car to make the short, twelve-mile trip to Tiverton.

He had booked seats for himself and Sandra and had also obtained tickets for them both. She arrived in good time, smiling, in a white dress that set off the tan she seemed to have acquired in the North Shields sun. She looked younger than her years, and a few heads turned as she walked towards him at the station. They made their way to the train and took their seats. She was carrying a small bag, as he was. An overnight stay would be necessary; they had booked rooms at a motel.

Eric's greeting was brusque enough for her to ask him, once they were settled in their compartment, 'Was everything all right? I mean, was there any trouble?'

'No problem,' he answered, but there had been. Anne had been furious. He supposed there was cause for her anger, in the sense that he had been unable to explain adequately why he had been persuaded to allow Sandra to accompany him to the West Country. Her presence was not necessary for him to interview Peter Stonier, and it had seemed to Anne that there was something clandestine afoot.

'I mean, dammit, Eric, can't you see what she's about?'

'Anne, you're exaggerating.'

'She just walks back into your life and you open your arms and accept her!'

'Now that's a stupid thing to say. There's no question of open arms. What we had was over years ago—'

'For you, maybe, but think of her and her situation! Her bloody husband goes charging off God knows where, and who does she turn to but you! There's enough damn lawyers about for her to go to, but she homes in on you, because you're the best? No, because she's out to make mischief, or else because she's still got an itch for you.'

Eric had smiled. It hadn't helped Anne's temper. 'You're overemphasizing my attraction—'

'Don't bloody patronize me, Eric Ward.' She stood waving an angry glass of whisky at him, her eyes flashing in temper, as beautiful as he had ever seen her. 'I'm not saying you're God's gift to women, I'm saying that *this* woman never wanted you when she had you and it just makes me damn suspicious when suddenly she *needs* you. She used you before, hurt you; has she changed that much? Maybe she's still using you; maybe she still wants to hurt you for the years that have gone past. Dammit—'

'You're overreacting, Anne. Try to be a bit more—'

'Mature? Is *that* what you were going to say? I tell you, you damn fool, this thing about our respective ages is just in your mind, and nobody else's, and I just hope that one day it isn't the stupidity that brings everything just crashing about our ears!'

She was right, of course. He had tried to deny her the privilege of concern and passion and jealousy. His own reaction had been coloured by the fact that he knew Sandra's presence with him was not strictly necessary. But when he had tried to explain to Anne, late that night, he hadn't been able to find the right words. So much for his experience and her immaturity. He wondered now, in the train, which of them was the fool.

There was still a short period to wait before the train pulled out and Eric realized he had forgotten to buy a newspaper. With a muttered explanation he left the compartment, made his way back over the footbridge and bought a daily paper at the bookstall. He walked back to the train slowly, newspaper tucked under his arm, oddly reluctant now to return to the compartment until the train was due to start. He hesitated on the platform, glancing up and down; small knots of people hurried forward to the train, seeking seats in compartments which were rapidly filling up, but one man, like Eric, seemed reluctant to board the train. He was standing half-hidden by one of the pillars, with his face averted from Eric, gazing towards the front compartments of the train. One hand was braced against the pillar; it was tanned, the fingers crooked, a cigarette dangling. Eric could not explain why his attention was drawn to the stranger except that he was aware, in spite of the casual nature of the stance, of a certain coiled tension in the man, as though he was searching for something, or someone.

Eric glanced at his watch and decided it was time to return to his seat. He walked past the pillar and the man moved, so that his back was turned to Eric as he drew on his cigarette, dropped it, ground it under his foot. Eric stepped up into the train and turned to close the door behind him, glancing back, and the man was walking towards a door in the next carriage. For one second their eyes met: Eric gained an impression of a cold, grey stare over which there was suddenly a vague confusion, and then the man had clambered aboard and was lost to view.

Eric had little to say for the first part of the journey; Sandra dozed, after a few desultory attempts to begin a conversation and he read his newspaper. Oddly enough, his mind drifted back from time to time to the man he had seen at Newcastle station; something about him had touched a wisp of memory, as though he had seen him before, but it was nothing on which he could seize. By the time he and Sandra made their way to the restaurant car, he had dismissed it from his mind.

The latter part of the journey passed quickly enough; Sandra talked, entertainingly, about episodes of her life in the States, reminiscing about some of the more curious encounters she had made as a companion. She was good company, and Eric began to warm to her, the defences Anne had caused him to raise beginning to thaw. Nevertheless, he was confirmed in his understanding that Sandra Crane was not the woman she had been when she was married to him. He was uncertain, even so, exactly how she had changed, except for a greater ease in her manner.

Much of that ease disappeared as they drew near Exeter. She was silent for the last half-hour of the journey, staring moodily out of the window, and when the train arrived at the station and Eric took hold of her arm to assist her from the carriage, the muscle was rigid with tension, iron under the thin material of her dress. There was a small group of people waiting outside the station at the taxi-rank and it was only after twenty minutes' delay that Eric and Sandra were able to get a taxi. That others were annoyed by the waiting was obvious as they drew away; Eric looked back through the rear window to note that some kind of altercation had broken out at the taxi-rank. A taxi-driver was getting out of his cab, gesturing towards a young couple and speaking to the man Eric had observed at Newcastle. He seemed angry. He turned, glared after the taxi which was bearing Eric and Sandra away from the station as though he considered the cab should have been his, and he ran his hand through his short, springy black hair in frustration before turning away. Next moment he was lost to sight as the taxi negotiated the statue raised by a grateful Victorian citizenry to Redvers Buller, an incompetent general and veteran of the South African wars.

Astride his imposing mount, General Sir Redvers Buller showed broad shoulders, a deep chest and a head held proudly; there was no hint of a similar swollen pride in Peter

Stonier although, like the Buller statue, he was deep-chested, well built, and about five-ten, rather shorter than Eric Ward. He was in his mid-forties, Eric guessed, fair-haired, greying at the temples, and had the slightly worried look of a nervous insurance salesman who feared he'd be unable to meet his monthly targets. His eyes were of a curiously bleached blue, his face was lean and tanned by the Devon sun and he had strong, certain hands that belied the quick uncertainty of his eyes. He wore a somewhat crumpled suit and a blue tie, slightly awry; his appearance, and rather careless dress, gave him a ruffled charm that Eric guessed would appeal to women. They'd also like the weakness of his mouth: it was something they would want to reach out and touch.

'Sandra?' His glance was puzzled, then warming, and he held out his hands, took her right hand, held it for a moment, smiling. Eric looked at his ex-wife, watching her carefully: there was a moment's hesitation, a slight nervousness, and then she smiled, squeezed Stonier's hand and said she was glad to see him. She introduced Eric.

'A solicitor?' Vague doubts churned in Stonier's eyes, and he looked about him. They were standing in the narrow forecourt of a garage and showroom; situated at the far end of the town, it was fronted by a row of small shops, but behind and along to their left was the first sweep of rising moorland, lifting above the slow-moving Exe. The showroom was not well stocked and the business did not seem prosperous. Stonier waved his hand. 'Maybe we'd better go inside.'

Eric had dismissed the taxi; the driver seemed to know Stonier and they had had a brief, cheerful conversation before the man had gone. Now, in the small office at the back of the showroom Peter Stonier settled them into hard-backed, rather uncomfortable chairs, put on an electric kettle to make a cup of coffee for each of them, and then sat down behind a battered, cigarette-scarred desk littered with paper. 'Well, it's good to see you, Sandra, but with a solicitor, now that's a different matter!'

It was meant to be jocular, but the statement was edged with nervousness. Eric looked about him. 'Is business good, Mr Stonier?'

'It could be better.' Stonier laughed, and it was a brittle sound. 'Damn sight better, in fact. Wrong end of town; wrong position.'

'Not well chosen,' Eric suggested, 'like the position you had in York.'

There was one brief flash, one moment when something other than nervousness appeared in Stonier's eyes, but it was gone before it could be evaluated; the man shrugged, glanced at Sandra, and said, 'It's all a matter of chance, of luck. You have to take what's available at the time. Since I took over this place on lease, other, better places have become available but . . .' He let the words die. 'But I don't imagine you'll have come here to see me to talk about my business prospects.'

'That's right,' Eric replied. 'We've really come to talk to you about Charles Crane.'

'*Charles*?' Peter Stonier stared at Eric for several seconds; curiously, Eric had expected him to look towards Sandra for an explanation, but he did not do so. He touched his lips with his tongue, but his glance was steady, and deliberate. 'Haven't had anything to do with Charles for a hell of a time. How do you think I can help?'

'When did you last see him?'

Stonier slitted his eyes, wrinkling his face in thought. 'The autumn of nineteen eighty, I guess. Around about then.'

'In York?'

'That's right.' Now he did turn his head, glance towards Sandra. 'Shortly before you came to see me, and we . . . talked.' He hesitated. 'What's this all about?'

'We're just trying to trace Charlie,' Sandra said in a level tone.

'You mean he never came back?'

The incredulity in his tone seemed to affect her; her mouth became uncertain. 'I haven't heard from him — or about him — since the day he walked out on me at York.'

'We wondered whether he might have been in contact with you,' Eric said.

Stonier shook his head. 'No. I tell you, when he left the business at York he caused me more than a little embarrassment. I mean, the carpet business was never a booming one where we were concerned, and it was on the point of folding, but lighting out the way he did, it meant I had to settle up and get out fast. I was able to raise a bit of cash — managed to give Sandra a share of some of it, seeing she was left alone like that, but I was pretty strapped.' He looked about him ruefully. 'Haven't managed to haul myself back very high since, have I?'

'Did you make any attempt to get in touch with Crane then, or later?' Eric asked.

Stonier stared at him, and his mouth grew nervous again. 'Well, no. You got to understand, when Charlie stepped out like that it was pretty obvious to me that he—' Stonier slipped an apologetic glance towards Sandra '—he wanted to get clear. He left behind him some obligations I had to sort out. That was okay. He left behind a . . . a wife. That was his business, not mine. But once I was clear, there was no way I wanted truck with Charlie again. I'm no great shakes as a businessman but Charlie was no better. He did his share, pushing our York operation to the wall.'

'In what way?'

Stonier could not meet Eric's glance for a moment. He shrugged, looked about him with a vaguely desperate air, and then said, 'Well, somehow he wasn't around too much. The business didn't rate too high with him. Why should I get in touch with him again? He'd have nothing to offer me. He'd cut loose; that was fine with me.'

'What do you mean, he wasn't around very much?'

Stonier was silent. He glanced towards Sandra almost in apology; she stared at him and then suddenly rose. 'We have rooms booked at the motel, Peter. Can you arrange to have me driven there, now?'

Stonier stood up. 'Of course. There's a lad, keeps the cars clean, that sort of thing — he can take you.'

She glanced coolly at Eric, gave him a faint, weary smile. 'I have a feeling,' she explained, 'you'll both be more at ease if I'm not here. I'll see you back at the motel, Eric.'

Stonier left the office with her, and went out into the forecourt. A young lad with a Mohican haircut and blue jeans was introduced, then walked away to one of the cars. Stonier had a brief conversation with Sandra, seemingly assuring her of something, then he shook hands and she left. When he returned to the office Stonier slumped in his chair, opened the deep drawer in his desk and took out a bottle of Scotch. 'Join me?'

'Not for me.'

'Sandra thinks maybe Charlie left her for some other woman.'

'You think that likely?'

Stonier shrugged. 'I wouldn't know. Doubt it. But that's why she left us together.' He poured a stiff level of Scotch into a smeared glass. 'Fellers together — they can talk about sex things. Her theory, not mine.'

'But it's not a sex thing you want to talk about, is it?' Eric asked quietly.

With a hint of sudden belligerence, Stonier said, 'Hold on, I don't *need* to talk about anything. You come here asking for help—'

'I think you *do* need to talk,' Eric interrupted. 'If only to explain about the lease.'

'What do you mean?'

'The business at York.'

There was a short silence. Stonier stared at Eric blankly and then something moved deep in his eyes. His glance slipped away, defensive, alarmed, and he took a long pull at his Scotch, topped the glass again from the half-empty bottle. Eric waited for a little while and then said, 'You lied when you told Sandra you hadn't been in contact with Charles Crane after he left that day.'

'No.'

'It had to be a lie. You must have made contact with Crane. Both your signatures appeared on a deed of assignment prepared by York solicitors. That deed was dated *after* Crane is supposed to have disappeared, no one knew where. You knew where he was.'

'You told Sandra this?' Stonier asked. He was playing for time, trying to think.

'Where did he go, Stonier? Where did you make contact with him?'

The phone jangled, cutting across the tension that had arisen in the small office. Stonier reached for it like a thirsty man for water, his glance flickering an apology to Eric that was as sincere as a politician's promise. 'Yes? Stonier here.'

Eric was unable to hear what was said, the speaker's voice garbled and hollowed by the phone cradled against Stonier's face. Eric stared at that face, trying to weigh up what he was seeing. There was something wrong about Peter Stonier, something unconvincing, but he could not put his finger on what it was. It was as though the car salesman was trying to distance himself from the questions he was being asked, standing back and weighing them in the balance of advantage. He was an observer, almost; a watcher — of Sandra, Eric, and even of himself. But not now. His face had stiffened, the muscles of his jaw tense, and apart from one swift, flickering glance at Eric, as though to check whether he could hear what was being said, he kept his eyes down to his desk.

'What did you say?' Stonier asked urgently. There was a brief gabble of sound, and Stonier nodded. 'I appreciate that . . . Look, would you mind staying out of the way? It could be important . . . We could meet, talk about it this evening . . . That's right.' There was again a brief gabbling, then Stonier nodded. 'I'll remember. That's right . . . I owe you, Fred.'

He replaced the receiver, stared at it for a moment then looked at Eric. It was possible Eric had been mistaken in his first summary of Peter Stonier: he was a harder man than he had at first realized.

'You were saying?' Stonier asked.

'You'd seen Crane.'

'No.'

'But the deed of assignment—'

Peter Stonier waved a hand abruptly, took another drink of Scotch and seemed to come to an abrupt decision. 'Look, you'd better understand the way it was. Sandra thinks he maybe left her for another woman. That's not the way I saw it. He was in trouble.'

'What kind of trouble?'

'You asked me why he wasn't around too much, at the carpet business in York. The fact was, he was into something else.'

'Such as?'

'I don't know.'

'You can do better than that, Stonier.'

'There are times when you don't sound like a solicitor.'

'I have a somewhat different background. It taught me to detect the odour of villainy when it's in the air.' Stonier pursed his lips, and raised one shoulder in an affected gesture of defeat. 'Maybe I can do better, as you say, but you got to understand I don't *know*, it's only guesswork on my part. The fact is, yes, I think Charlie Crane was involved in something that was shady.'

'Why?'

'We'd set up a carpet business and it wasn't doing well, but I had an idea about expansion. Charlie wasn't interested. For some reason he wanted to stay in York, where he was. It was the first sniff I got that maybe he had reasons to work the business, but not seriously — just to keep him in pocket money or . . .'

'Yes?'

'As a front.'

Eric took a slow, deep breath. 'A front for what, Stonier?'

'That's where guesswork becomes just that. I've no idea. All I can tell you is that Charlie was away on regular trips, once a month. Never said where he was going; told me he wanted to tramp the circuit, seek out carpet buyers, orders, contacts. Never came back with anything substantial, but what business he did pull came in from the same three areas. Manchester, Middlesbrough and Newcastle.'

'I still can't see what you are driving at.'

'The number of orders he brought back were few,' Stonier explained. 'The kind of thing a *part-time* road man might pull. But they gave him a *reason* to be in these areas, you know what I mean? And a cover, if any questions were asked in due course.'

'By you?'

'By *anyone*.' Stonier leaned forward, confidentially. 'Look, Mr Ward, I don't know the answers. But my guess is Charlie was tied up with something crooked. It took him to those three towns. It got him out on the road. York was a convenient centre to reach all three places; the business was a legitimate cover to travel. But his lifestyle wasn't paid for by our business. And when he decamped, he really decamped. Like he was scared.'

'Of whom?'

'You tell me. But he lit out so fast he didn't even have time to settle up with me. He took the company car, you know, I put a trace on it, but it never turned up. I think he was scared about something, under pressure, and he just dropped out of sight.'

'With some efficiency, it would seem,' Eric murmured.

'That's the way of it,' Stonier said, with an air of satisfaction.

'Why didn't you go to the police?' Eric asked sharply.

Alarm twisted Stonier's mouth and he wriggled in his chair. 'Didn't seem necessary at the time.'

'Not good enough, Stonier. You say you think he was scared, under pressure. He disappeared, leaving you to deal with a business in trouble. You've never heard from him since. Didn't you think — if you guessed he'd been involved with something shady — that he might have been murdered?'

'I don't know—'

'Why didn't you contact the police?' Eric persisted.

'Because—' Stonier shook his head in anger, whether simulated or real, Eric could not tell. 'Because all I had was

. . . guesswork. There was nothing really to go on. I didn't know who he was involved with. And if I'd gone to the police there would have been questions, rooting around — I just didn't want to be bothered with all that crap. Crane had gone; good riddance to him. I wanted a clean start. I got away from the area, came down here, tried starting up again. All right, I've made no great shakes of it, but it's a living! I couldn't have done that, maybe, if I'd had the police thundering on my door all hours of the day and night.'

'It would have come to that? If they'd investigated Charles Crane?'

'How the hell do I know?' Truculence stained his tone. 'I just didn't want to get involved.'

Eric paused, watching Stonier carefully. 'The deed of assignment, signed by you and Crane. If you had had no contact with Crane after the time he left . . .'

'All right, all right!' Stonier said passionately. 'I didn't see Charlie. I had no way of contacting him, didn't know where he was, and the bloody solicitors told me that his signature was required on the deed of assignment. Look, he'd buggered me about, you know? He'd never done his whack in the business; always motoring off somewhere or other; I was left to haul the whole thing in, and I needed the money from the assignment, needed it to come down here, make a fresh start, try to *get* somewhere! I *deserved* that cash, and *she* deserved some of it too, after the way he'd left her high and dry.'

'That's really why you didn't go to the police, isn't it?' Eric asked quietly.

'You work it out,' Stonier said bitterly.

'If you had, it might have come out that one of the signatures on the deed of assignment had been forged. *You'd* written in both signatures.'

'Forgery,' Stonier said with a sneer in his voice, 'used to be a hanging offence, didn't it?'

* * *

The dining-room in the motel was fairly crowded but the waiter was able to find a table for Eric and Sandra in a quiet corner where they were able to feel relatively private. Eric was not certain whether she had spoken to the man before they came down to dinner; it may have been that their separate rooms and dining together had raised his curiosity. Perhaps he saw himself as a sexual pathfinder, with a large tip as his own objective. The table was certainly intimately situated; Sandra's knee touched his lightly.

'How well did you know Stonier?' Eric asked abruptly.

Her hesitation was brief, but considered. 'We met a few times socially, with Charles. Stonier was — and it seems still is — a bachelor. No family we ever heard of, bit of a loner really. He was basically a business acquaintance who didn't make very many social demands.'

'But he was helpful after Charles left.'

'He was helpful.' She smiled a half-secret smile. 'I told you — I thought he was . . . interested. Still is, I suspect, from the way he said goodbye.'

'There's something wrong about him,' Eric said flatly. 'What did Charles tell you about him?'

'Very little. Charles talked very little about his business; in fact I really didn't know where he made his money. Not from the carpet operation, it would seem. But then, Charles talked very little anyway. I often used to wonder, after we married, what it was he wanted from me. Maybe a decorative companion. The possessiveness would turn to sex from time to time, when the north wind blew, of course. When it blew really cold, inevitably, *he* blew.'

'You're suddenly sounding very cynical about Crane.'

'He left me.'

'Not for another woman, it seems.'

'Stonier told you that?' She shrugged indifferently. 'In a way it makes no sense, either way, nor does it matter. Did you get much useful from Peter?'

'He suggests your husband was in trouble. Involved in something shady.'

She was silent for a little while, then she sipped her wine. 'I wouldn't know about that. I was an . . . incurious wife.'

'As he would seem to have been an incurious partner. As I said, there's something out of key with Stonier. I don't trust him.'

Sandra's knee brushed against his lightly as she leaned forward. In the dim light her eyes seemed large, deep in colour. 'If he can't help, he can't help.'

'Yes, but I'm not certain he's told me all he really knows. I had a curious feeling about him as he talked. You know those old movies, the ones made in the 'thirties? They had certain conventions about acting; you could tell how things were going to turn out by the gestures, the patterns of speech, the eyeball rolling.' Eric hesitated. 'I got something of that impression with Stonier.'

'He rolled his eyeballs?'

Eric laughed. 'No, of course not. But he seemed to be . . . standing back. Watching himself, noting my reactions, stage-managing something. Acting, even. It was some kind of a performance, some kind of stage setting.'

'You've now cast him as actor, manager and props man. I think we should just forget him, for tonight, at least.'

Eric glanced at her. She had taken several glasses of wine; he had sipped at a martini before dinner but had drunk no other alcohol. The liquor would seem to have warmed her; she was looking at him now with a disturbing directness. 'I'm still trying to find your husband, Sandra. In some way, I think Stonier has more to tell us—'

'I'd rather you told me what you have in mind.'

'What about?'

'The rest of the evening.'

He paused, his glance on the rim of her wineglass. 'We'd better get something clear—'

'Did you ever love me, Eric? Why did you marry me? When you caught me that day I know you thought I was a whore. I suppose I was. I've changed, somewhat. And now I've got someone who cares for me, and who I'll marry as soon as this sordid business is over and done with. But he's a long way from here, and there are distant sounds I can hear from way back, things you once said to me, things I made you say—'

'Sandra—'

'Will you join me tonight?'

'No.'

'Because of that rich little wife of yours?'

'That's only one reason.'

'I have a feeling I won't enjoy hearing the others.' She sipped her wine reflectively. 'You always were, in a funny sort of way, a heartless bastard. Proper, in control, and concerned to do the right thing. Principle, isn't it? Not like me. Flesh rules, OK? With you, something else rules. Never figured it out. Never did . . .'

When she had left him and gone to her room he sat in the darkness of his own room and thought about what she had said. She claimed she did not understand him . . . perhaps that girl on the *Alouette* did not understand him either, when she had felt his body move and yet he had rejected her. It was odd, that: a butterfly of calculation touched his mind, fluttering away, elusive. Within days he had had two attractive women offering themselves to him, and he had rejected them both. Catherine and Sandra, they had had something in common apart from the rejection, but for the life of him he could not think what it was.

He was tired. It had been an unsatisfactory trip. Anne had been right. He had been wrong to come; wrong to bring Sandra with him.

The butterfly flickered in and out of his consciousness as he tried to sleep. When sleep finally came, it had still not alighted.

* * *

Eddie Stevens had been busy.

It looked as though his involvement with the badger story and his subsequent discovery of the corpse at Rothbury

Crags had persuaded the powers that be that they had an interesting and useful property on their hands: a journalist to whom things *happened*. It was a valuable commodity, all agreed: newspapermen often made things happen, even manufactured news, but it was far more valuable to have a talent for being at the place where things happened spontaneously. The spark could become a conflagration in the right hands, a journalistic bushfire. So Eddie had been asked down to the London office for a chat about his future plans.

They had been suitably impressed. He'd suggested it would be useful if he maintained an interest in the Crags body, for he had a feeling it could blow soon, and since he'd been in at the beginning, if one could call death a beginning . . . One could, they gravely assured him, in newspaper terms.

And then there was the Halliday Arthur Lansley matter. Sage heads nodded, with only a hint of a doubt, as he talked. Lansley was, after all, old hat, yesterday's news, stale as a petrified Bath bun. But if he thought there was still mileage in it, they were prepared to listen, particularly if he really could link Lansley to the drugsmuggling gangs in the North-East, and point to the smoke signals of police corruption. A byline on a series, maybe, in one of their second-stable Sundays of course, to start, but if he reeled in some really big mackerel . . .

The key could be this solicitor, Eric Ward. Eddie Stevens had a feeling about him too. Straight, difficult to move off a given line, but he had a contact with Lansley and there was something about him that seemed to have triggered a happy response in the old reprobate at La Canebière. He was willing to talk to Ward, and that was more than the old bastard was prepared to do with the gentlemen of the press.

So, armed with the chainmail of approval from the Board, Eddie Stevens had sallied forth and pushed his luck with a number of northern editors and reporters. He'd talked to wharf-rats off Newcastle Quay, and pimps at Sunderland Dock. He'd spent two solid days — and nights — in the crowded seedy heartland of Middlesbrough red light areas, and he'd had an Irish Rebel night at the Tyneside Irish club, shamrocks, shillelaghs, Guinness and grimacing. There had been five solid hours talking to an ex-City Leader who still defended his political actions as he sat in the narrow, crowded front room of his semi-detached house in Duke Street, a bottle of Newcastle Brown Ale in his hand, feet encased in worn red slippers and a striped, collar-less shirt shining grubbily in the dim light of his overshadowed windows.

Eddie had been very busy, but it had all come to nothing.

Lansley *was* yesterday's news. No one was very interested in him now. His contacts in the North-East, men he had been much involved with in business enterprises, hardly seemed to remember him — or at least, affected not to remember him. The Quayside had given him nothing on the drug connection; the Teesside connection would appear to have been broken; it was all a reminiscing about the old days of the late 'seventies, with nothing seeming to move in the present. Crime, it seemed, of the kind Eddie was looking for, was a stagnant pond topped by innocent ducks. No one had anything to say because no one had anything to say.

The members of the Board in London were displaying no impatience. Yet. Eddie watched his expense account with a little more care and tried to marshal his facts. Both were looking distinctly more meagre as time went on.

And Eric Ward was no help. Two brief conversations on the phone, each as distant and unhelpful as the other. Ward, it seemed, was busy too, and didn't have time to talk with Eddie Stevens. It was a time for an oozing away of confidence, the drain of excitement into a sludge of doubt.

It was then that Superintendent Charnley rang.

Eddie had not had a great deal to do with the uniformed branch at Superintendent level. They tended to become administrative animals, non-practising policemen in his experience, content to do a PR job, reminisce about their times on the beat, and scare the hell out of their juniors in the office.

Charnley was something different.

Eddie had met him several times and remembered him as a big, heavy man who moved like a cat and smiled like one — feline charm, edged with contempt. He was a Tynesider who'd spent twelve years serving his police apprenticeship in the tougher parts of Liverpool; he'd come back, won swift promotion at Newcastle, and somehow seemed to have a finger on the pulse of every criminal activity in the North. He had a face like a sagging pudding, heavy-jowled and ponderous, but his eyes were sharp and expressive, needle points that could dig into a man's conscience and hidden fears. He had bad skin, mottled as his temper, but his judgment was as fine as the hairs on the back of his huge hands.

His was not an invitation a journalist worth his salt turned down. Charnley did not waste his time with hacks.

* * *

The meeting place was a surprise. The White Swan stood at the edge of the country road, surrounded by fields but subjected to the regular thunder of jets landing at Newcastle Airport just five miles distant. The interior of the pub was almost as sparsely furnished as the car park and its base nowhere near as solid: the floor was timber, its joints sprung and squeaking when a customer of any weight entered. The clientele was of the affected kind and not to Eddie's taste: denim-suited, gold earrings, condescending tones and accents that were artificial and cracked on occasional flat vowel sounds. Charnley stood out like a sore thumb, cheerful, tweed jacket and cavalry twill a concession to the locals, but his heavy face shining and his thinning red hair horridly bristling on his damp scalp.

'This your local?' Eddie Stevens asked disbelievingly.

'Got a cottage up the road. Aunt left it to me. Live alone, you know. Like to see how the other half think they'd like to live.'

'You come here to observe?'

'Sneer. Pint?'

Stevens nodded. 'Please.'

Charnley returned, affably bearing two pints, and sat down in the corner with Stevens. He raised his glass. 'Cheers.'

'And you.' Stevens sipped his beer. 'This is a surprise. Seeing you in mufti and all.'

'A privilege available to few. A compliment, from me to you, a gesture to the brave men of the press.'

'Brave?'

'Always been an admirer, I have.' The heavy pudding face leered confidentially at Stevens. 'I mean, all that prurient sniffing around boudoirs — running the gauntlet of angry husbands and lovers. But more to the point, the war correspondents. William Howard Russell.'

'What?'

'Another surprise for you. Didn't know I was a Crimean War buff did you?' Charnley took a long pull at his beer. 'It's where I first gained my admiration of the press. Thought you were a load of creeps till I realized that Russell — the first of the war correspondents — laid his life on the line in the pursuit of truth. Like you.'

'Like me?' Stevens was unable to dampen the dry rasp of alarm in his voice.

'Certainly, Eddie my boy. Rothbury Crags. I mean, you laid it on the line there, didn't you, in pursuit of truth.'

'It was only a badger hunt, for God's sake,' Eddie mumbled, feeling vaguely aware of being laughed at.

'But you got smashed about a bit, didn't you?' The big policeman chuckled. 'Like you might again, like.'

'What do you mean?'

'News not been released yet, but it'll be on the bulletins at nine o'clock.'

'What?'

'Careless buggers, those lads at Durham. I mean, letting him jump the van, when they were in transit.'

'What the hell are you on about?'

Superintendent Charnley smiled complacently, but his button eyes were watchful, and sharp. 'Frank Penry. They were transferring him to Durham. He jumped it, this afternoon. They never laid a finger on him. I thought you ought to be among the first to know.'

Eddie Stevens's throat was dry. 'Why?'

'The things he's been saying since he was put inside, a week ago. Like if he ever got his hands on you . . . Like I say, I admire you chaps. Put it on the line, you do, in the interests of right and justice.'

Eddie Stevens scowled at his beer. He was finding the superintendent's heavy humour rather too much to bear. 'Is that why you asked me to meet you in this . . . dump?'

Charnley smiled expansively, to denote that he took no offence at the implied criticism. 'Among other things. I thought we in the service owed it to you, to give a warning. Penry sounded serious; we think you ought to lock your doors at night for a while. Until we catch him again. That might take a while. He's got friends; the badger boys stick together; country folk tend to be a bit independent.' He paused, eyeing Stevens thoughtfully. 'On the other hand, you've not been spending too much time at that flat of yours recently, have you?'

'What's that supposed to mean?'

'You been talking to people, asking questions, like.'

'That's my job,' Stevens replied cautiously.

'That's right. Putting it on the line, Eddie, putting it on the line.'

'You've got your own nightlines, obviously.'

'Ah, come on, boy, it's not only poachers land the big ones! We're both in the business of information — you for your purposes, me for mine. It just so happens, when I've pulled in a few little wriggling trout recently, they tell me that you've been fishing pretty heavy along the banks of Tyne and Wear.'

'What do you want, Superintendent Charnley?' Eddie asked directly.

'Just what's making you tick, Mister Stevens.'

'I'm a journalist, Charnley.'

'Interested in yesterday's news?'

'Ah . . . Halliday Arthur Lansley.'

'That's about the size of it.'

'Why are you so curious?'

'Why are you so curious, Eddie?' Charnley leaned back in his seat, contemplating the half-empty pint glass in front of him. 'The pity is, you don't know enough to talk to the right people. Like the police.'

'I thought—'

'That we wouldn't give you the information you wanted? But we're public servants! You should have come to us, Eddie, asked us your questions. You might have got answers faster, and more accurate.'

'Supposing,' Stevens said cautiously, 'I started asking now?'

'Fire away.'

'Halliday Arthur Lansley . . . was he involved in drug smuggling in the North-East?'

'We are pretty certain he was. No direct proof, of course. Not enough to send him up for a long stretch anyway — not that it's important in any case, state of health he's in.'

'He's healthy enough — and rich enough — to enjoy the south of France.'

'You score a point. What else do you want to know?'

'Was there a police cover-up, a deal — that left him with just a tax evasion charge?'

Charnley finished his drink, rose to his feet, and bought himself another pint. He did not bring one for Stevens. The journalist recognized the signs, and waited. When he spoke, Charnley's affability had become less obvious, a cutting edge entering his tone. 'Cover-up, deals, that's the kind of loose journalistic language that doesn't go down well with . . . public servants. Let's put it like this, Eddie. We had . . . evidence, of a sort, that tied our friend Lansley in with all sorts of deals. Some of it would stick, the rest . . . Well, in any operation of that kind you have to take the rough with the smooth, let one villain get away with something so you can close down a bigger operation. All right, we reached an arrangement with Lansley, that was mutually beneficial. In return for certain information he supplied to us, we agreed not to press certain charges.'

'So he copped only the minor offence?'

'Something like that. Of course, we also knew he was a pretty sick man at the time, and wasn't likely to give us a full pound of flesh anyway. One has,' he added with conscious irony, 'to display a certain amount of humanity on these occasions, after all. But you have other questions, about other people.'

'Such as?'

'Donald Bartlett.'

'How—'

'Oh, come on, Stevens, do you think the police sit in Panda cars playing cards all day? We have men on the *beat*; they hear things. While you've been rabbiting on about getting information concerning Lansley, drugs, police corruption, you've also once or twice asked some characters if they can give you information about one Donald Bartlett. Like I said — you should have come to us.'

'What can you tell me about him?'

Charnley smiled with a hint of unpleasantness. 'You picked a right one to ask questions about. Bartlett is one of your original tearaways. He was in the Army as a boy soldier, and learned a few nasty tricks during his ten years there. Got involved with the hammering of a sergeant in his unit in Germany, was sent home for a period in the glasshouse, then got out. A natural bent for crime and violence put him in with the right characters, and his inability to distinguish between acceptable and dirty crime pushed him into the drug scene.'

'He worked for Lansley?'

'An aberration. Lansley, in my view, was never into the kind of strong-arm stuff that Bartlett existed for. But from time to time Lansley, however distasteful it might have been for him, needed muscle — the kind Bartlett could provide. They made uneasy bedfellows, is my guess, but, yes, Lansley employed Bartlett for a while. The pity was, we never managed to nail Bartlett for something heavy. We did get him, of course. But only a three-year stretch, for assault and battery. I had a couple of sessions with him, in fact. He's a hard man. Character to be avoided. Character not to ask questions about. Particularly just now.'

'Why now?'

Charnley smiled to himself, satisfied. 'He finished his stretch. No remission. He got out, about two months ago.'

Eddie Stevens finished his drink and rose shakily to his feet. He gestured towards the half-empty beer glass in front of the police superintendent. Charnley shook his head. 'No, thanks. I got to be careful who I'm beholden to.' Stevens ordered a large whisky and took it back to the table where Charnley sat waiting. He sipped his whisky silently for a while. It was Charnley who broke the silence. 'You see, Eddie, it pays to talk to the coppers. All this charging around on expense accounts: waste of time. Talk to the horse's mouth.'

'It won't always talk back.'

'There are times, there are times. You got to remember, just as you got plans for your future, so do we. A sort of grand design, you know? Trouble is, how do you start knitting the pattern of it all . . . ?'

'I don't understand what—'

'You must surely be asking yourself why I've taken the trouble to talk to you this way, Eddie? I mean, we could have left you fuddling around the whorehouses and fast bars, getting gossip and paying through the nose for it and nothing you could print. Still nothing though, is there? But the information *is* hard. Penry's out and gunning for you; Bartlett's out; Bartlett was tied in with Lansley; Lansley did get a deal with us on the understanding he helped us control the drug supply entries.'

'So why *are* you talking to me?' Eddie asked, nervous and exasperated.

Almost dreamily, Charnley said, 'A study of history, man, that's where it's all at. You know, I always felt there was a great injustice done regarding the Crimea. Cardigan and his bloody fool action, charging the guns with the Light Brigade, it got all the glory, all the write-ups, when a far greater action had already occurred. Finest charge in the whole of cavalry history: the Heavy Brigade, slicing right through the Russian horde, with Campbell in the lead. It happened only minutes earlier. It got forgotten.'

'What the hell has Balaclava got to do with me?' Eddie snarled.

'Lessons of history, man. Don't get blinded by stupid actions, by noise and thunder and glory. Read behind it; work out why people act as they do! Cardigan had his motives, and one of them was sheer jealousy, sheer frustration at seeing Campbell boiling into the Russians and him, Cardigan, seeing no action!'

'So?'

'So why are you asking about Lansley and Bartlett at *this* time in particular?'

Eddie Stevens stared at him in exasperation. 'What's so particular about this time?'

'I want to know why you're chasing these names.'

'You *know* why!'

'I don't. Not just *now*. I think you have information I don't have, and—' Charnley's eyes were cold — 'I intend to get that information.'

'This is why you've been talking to me — trading information.' Eddie Stevens nodded. 'All right. But what the hell is it you want?'

Charnley took a long pull at his beer, finishing it. He wiped his hand delicately against his mouth. 'I want you to tell me everything you know about a man called Charles Edward Crane.'

CHAPTER 4

1

Mr Justice Stepford's impatience was legendary. It was an impatience that tended to show in his septuagenarian face: his narrow lips twisted as though he was biting into a fresh lemon and his grey, wispy eyebrows drew closer together in a disapproving line the longer the legal argument went on. Sheridan Enterprises had been ill-advised in their choice of counsel: a flamboyant company lawyer was the wrong man to face the traditionally-minded Stepford, and as the hearing extended into the afternoon session and the old judge began to wriggle in discomfort, Eric knew that things were swinging their way. He had told Anne so at lunchtime, but by four in the afternoon, Stepford had had enough, and said so.

'The subject-matter in dispute is land based in Mexico, the El Centro property. As a result of dealings between Morcomb Estates and one Halliday Arthur Lansley an equitable charge was created over that property. The property was then transferred to Sheridan Enterprises and it is this company which now, as defendants in this hearing, point out that the charge is void by Mexican law, for want of registration.'

The grey eyebrows grew even closer together as the judge leaned forward to peer more closely at the affidavits in front of him. 'Mr Lansley agrees in his statement to this hearing — though I am sorry that Mr Lansley sees fit to refuse to attend the hearing personally — that the transfer to Sheridan Enterprises was "subject to any mortgage, charge or lien now existing". The Sheridan company argues that this is irrelevant, given the Mexican requirement for registration.'

He paused, and the room was silent. The hearing was taking place in judge's chambers rather than an open courtroom and took the appearance of a business meeting rather than legal proceedings. Nevertheless, the small group of antagonists were aware of the tension that had arisen during the course of the long day, and the light breeze that now filtered in through the open window did nothing to relieve the atmosphere. Eric glanced at Anne, absorbed in what the judge was saying.

'It has been objected, at this hearing to adjudicate on whether the equitable charge in favour of Morcomb Estates can be enforced, that the Sheridan company cannot be so enforced because there was no privity of obligation between the debenture holders of Sheridan Enterprises, Inc. and the directors of Morcomb Estates plc. It was not the Sheridan company who made the charge and under Mexican law they remain the absolute and unfettered owners of the land, subject to no charge. Such is their argument.'

In the brief pause that followed, Eric whispered to Anne, 'Here it comes.'

'I face no difficulty,' Mr Justice Stepford said decisively, 'in disposing of this argument. When Sheridan took the El Centro property they agreed to take it subject to an express obligation in favour of Morcomb Estates. Mexican law, the *lex situs,* the law of the country in which the land is situated, says the charge is void for want of registration. It is clearly unconscionable, however, that Sheridan should rely exclusively upon the *lex situs* in this matter. I am persuaded by the precedent quoted in *Mercantile Investment v. River Plate Trust,* and consequently I find for Morcomb Estates . . .'

Counsel for the American company was quickly on his feet. Stepford raised an irritated hand. 'I know. You will wish to appeal. Mr Ward . . . I wish to see you in chambers in twenty minutes.'

Mr Justice Stepford, refreshed by a cup of tea, was a little more relaxed, but not a great deal so when Eric presented himself at chambers twenty minutes later. The judge did not invite him to take a seat, nor did he take one himself; rather, he marched about the room, brushing against the heavy curtains of the windows as he passed, expressing his displeasure.

'This has been a messy business, Mr Ward, and I'm not convinced it has been properly dealt with. There is every possibility that this judgment can be overturned on appeal, and I'm getting too old to enjoy having my judgments reversed.'

'If I may say so, sir, I thought—'

'I don't give a damn what you think,' Stepford interrupted testily. 'Let me tell you what *I* think. There's something that smells in this case — and I know this man Lansley's reputation. All judges aren't born fools! In an issue such as the one we've dealt with today there is always the question of personal obligation. The *River Plate Trust* case, as you'll know, arose under the doctrine laid down in *Penn v. Baltimore.* Exceptional circumstances, Mr Ward; equity arising out of personal obligation. But what about fraud, hey? What about fraud?'

'I don't quite follow.'

The old man's little eyes gleamed. 'Land in Mexico, transfer of shareholdings, the timing of the transfers . . . and this man Lansley. Are you certain it was all above board? Did he have a personal stake, undeclared, in this American company?'

'I had an assurance—'

'Assurance my backside! I don't like having my judgments overturned — and this one could be! But not if there's fraud involved. Don't take assurances, Mr Ward *check!* And do it fast, if you want to avoid heavy costs on your client's part!'

On the steps outside the building, Eric explained to Anne what Stepford had said. It was clear the testy old man had accepted the arguments Eric had raised, but recognized that since there was an equity involved and the case was a finely balanced one, there was a strong possibility of it being overturned. The consequences could be expensive; unless there was an out of court settlement, legal proceedings could drag on with Sheridan Enterprises winning in the end. The clue, as far as Stepford was concerned, lay in the question of possible fraud.

'If we can show that Lansley still has a personal interest in the whole business we can probably persuade Sheridan to drop their defence. But it'll need some hard checking—'

'And you'll need to see Lansley again,' Anne suggested.

'I think so.'

She glanced at him curiously. 'You never did give me much detail about this yacht trip you had with him.'

'There wasn't a great deal to tell.'

'*Eric?*'

He turned at the sound of the voice, and something moved in his chest. It was absurd to feel guilty for he had nothing to feel guilty about but when he saw Sandra Crane standing near the pillared entrance to the hallway he was acutely aware of Anne's presence beside him.

'Sandra? Are you all right?'

She was pale, and was obviously disturbed. She came forward, held out her hand as though for support and he took it. Beside him Anne moved slightly. He turned, glanced at her and said, 'This is Sandra Crane. Sandra, my wife Anne.'

She hardly seemed to be aware of what he said; she stared at him blankly, her mouth set. 'I'd like to talk to you.'

Anne was cool, and quite controlled. She smiled slightly, but there was an edge of ice to it. 'I'll see you later, Eric. I can make my own way back.'

Eric hesitated, but Anne was already walking away down the steps. He turned back to Sandra, and asked, 'What's the matter?'

'It's Charles.'

'Charles Crane?'

She nodded. 'They've found him.'

'To be more precise,' a man's voice cut across them, '*I* found him. That time up at Rothbury Crags.'

* * *

They took a taxi down to the Quayside and Eric's office. Once there, with a cup of coffee in her hands, Sandra seemed more controlled, less shaky, and Eric was able to question Eddie Stevens's presence.

'It's two days since,' the reporter said easily, 'that I had a long discussion with one Superintendent Charnley. Tough old nut, that one. But quite helpful, really. He told me they had been working on the body up at Rothbury Crags and had got nothing from the clothing, teeth and so on. So they went back and sifted the area again, and at last they came up with a gold ring. It seems the ring was inscribed . . .'

Sandra's head lowered, and she sipped at her coffee.

Stevens went on. 'Anyway, it took them a while to get the traces out, but they finally ran down the fact that there was a Charles Edward Crane had been in business in York, and that he'd had a wife and all that. So she was pulled in today for identification purposes.'

'Were you able to identify him?' Eric asked.

She nodded, but said nothing.

'My interest in the case — having found the body in the first instance — meant I was out there when the identification took place. I was talking to one of the coppers — bloke called Jennings, you may recall him. Told me he remembered Mrs Crane from way back. Said she'd once been married to you.'

'So you detected a human interest story,' Eric said sarcastically.

Stevens touched the faint bruise on his face thoughtfully. 'Well, you could say that. But there's a bit more to it than just that. Of course, ex-wife of ex-copper, now solicitor, getting her second husband murdered, makes a story, doesn't it'

'Stevens—' Eric warned.

'No, don't get me wrong! I'm not that heartless. I want to help.'

'In what way?'

'Crane was murdered, after all! I guess Mrs Crane here — and you too for that matter — will want to get your hands on the character who killed him!'

Sandra Crane put down her cup. She looked up to Eric, ignoring the reporter. 'I never thought it would be like this, when I came to you. His disappearing the way he did, I just thought . . . I never really questioned it . . . I never thought it would be like this.'

Gently Eric touched her shoulder. 'Don't worry, the police will find out who was responsible.'

'I don't care.'

Eric glanced towards Stevens standing casually near the window, and warned her, 'Sandra, I don't think this is the time—'

'No, let me say it,' she muttered fiercely. 'I *don't* care! You know perfectly well that things had been breaking up between Charles and me before he walked out. When he left me, it ended, it was over as far as I was concerned. He left me, and I no longer wanted to know — and in the period since, I've come to accept I would never see him again. So the fact that he's dead . . .' A flash of defiance came over her. 'That sounds hard, doesn't it, but it's the truth! He was murdered — all right, but that makes no difference as far as I'm concerned. I don't know why he was killed, or where or how, and I don't want to know. As for who killed him, I don't give a damn about that either! He had his own, secret existence I knew nothing about, and it's no time for me to be asking questions now.'

'Sandra, you're upset,' Eric said quietly. 'Just hold on for a moment while Mr Stevens leaves—'

'There's no need,' she insisted. 'I'm leaving. All right, I was upset, shaken, and Mr Stevens offered to bring me to you. He clearly has business with you, but I don't want to know. Charles is dead, but he died for me a long while ago. Now, I have what I need.'

'You have what you need?' Eric repeated.

'The proof I asked you to get for me,' she said in a hard, bitter tone. 'There's nothing to stop me making the claim now, Eric, so you can get the papers ready for me. I won't need to bother you again, once that's done. I can start all over again, and forget Charles, this whole business — even you.' She stood up, hesitated, staring at him as though wanting to say something more, but then she nodded, and walked past him to the door.

'Where will I be able to contact you?' he asked.

'I'll be in touch, in a couple of days.'

Eddie Stevens expelled his breath after she had gone, and perched himself on the edge of Eric's desk. He nodded in appreciation. 'Gutsy lady.'

'What is it you want?'

'What did she mean, saying she's got what she needs now her old man's proved dead?'

Eric sat down behind his desk. 'I don't think that it's something she would want me to discuss with you. I ask again, what do you want with me?'

Eddie Stevens shrugged. 'I'm not quite sure, Mr Ward. You'll recall I asked you to act for me in the assault matter — you heard, by the way that they still haven't caught that bastard Penry?'

'I heard he'd escaped from police custody.'

'He'd been mouthing about getting another crack at me,' Stevens said with a lopsided grin, 'but I reckon he'll be more concerned with keeping low than seeking me out.'

'You were saying . . .'

'Of course. Yes, I asked you to act in the assault case, but I had another motive, as you'll recall. The Lansley story.'

'I don't think you can help yourself much by expecting material from me.'

'Don't be so short, Mr Ward! It's whether I can give you anything. What happened at the hearing today?' Briefly, a shade reluctantly, Eric explained. The reporter nodded thoughtfully, frowning as he was led through the legal niceties of the judgment. 'So it's back to Lansley again,' he said finally. 'Well, there you are.'

'Where are we?'

Stevens stood up, walked around the room with his hands locked behind his back, self-important, confident. 'It's like this. My finding Crane's corpse up at Rothbury Crags has given me some clout with my employers. The badger story, I mean, that was really pretty small beer, but they liked the way I rolled over and came up with a cadaver, you know?'

'Newspapers have curious views of behaviour,' Eric said grimly.

'The fact is,' Stevens said positively, 'I've got connections now which I can use, maybe to your benefit.'

'In what way?'

'You want to check whether Lansley is tied in personally with Sheridan Enterprises. You've already had difficulty in making a check: I have sources that may be able to dig deeper.'

Eric leaned back in his chair and observed Stevens carefully. 'All right. So you'll do some work for me. I imagine it'll be at a price.'

'Everything has a price, Mr Ward.'

'And yours?'

'Pressure on Halliday Arthur Lansley.'

'What sort of pressure can I bring?'

Stevens nodded, considering. 'I'm not sure. But let's take this Sheridan case. Lansley was helpful, wasn't he? Okay, maybe he was keeping something back, but he was helpful. He was prepared to see you. He wanted something from you.'

'Information about this man Bartlett, whether he's been seen on Tyneside.'

'Seems very little. I'd have thought Lansley would have wanted more than that. You sure he's not using you in some other way?'

Eric shrugged. 'I can't imagine how. But you haven't told me how I can put pressure on the man.'

'Well, let's assume there is something he wants from you; let's assume he is using you. Maybe he'll do a trade for further information.'

'On what?'

'On his activities a few years back.'

Eric smiled and shook his head. 'You still pursuing the drug-smuggling thing? Lansley is never going to admit to anything that will put further criminal charges over his head.'

'I agree. But on the assumption he wants something from you . . . Look, the fact is, I think there's a story in all this that could be big for me. I'm not sure what it is, but there's something going on I don't know about and you don't know about, but there are people around who are more than a little nervous.'

'Such as?'

'Superintendent Charnley.'

Eric was silent for a moment, then he leaned forward and picked up the phone, calling Frances at reception. 'Can you make us a couple of cups of tea?'

The two men remained silent for several minutes, Eric staring out of the window, Stevens still perched, leg swinging on the edge of his desk. Frances came in, saying hadn't they been lucky because the kettle was already boiling, and after she'd gone Eric looked thoughtfully at the reporter. 'Charnley.'

Stevens smiled thinly. 'Funny thing. Lansley is helpful to you; my cynical mind tells me he wants something from you. A senior copper like Charnley, he's suddenly more than helpful to me. So what does *he* want?'

'Tell me.'

'Information about one Charles Edward Crane.'

Eric sipped his tea and was silent. After a little while the reporter went on, 'You see, it's all very odd. I find this corpse up at Rothbury Crags. The forensic people finally come up with something that'll clinch an identity - though I wonder about that ring, you know? I mean, why didn't they find it on the first sifting? Bloody incompetence is probably the answer. Anyway, they get the identification, they check him out, and they finally pull in Mrs Crane — but only after friend Charnley arranges to meet me, talks openly about Lansley and Bartlett, and having given me the old friendly chat, asks some cagey questions about Crane.'

'What did he tell you about Bartlett?' Eric asked.

'Basically that he's a dangerous animal with a strong criminal tendency and somewhat addicted to violence. And, that he occasionally strong-armed for Lansley.'

'So why is Lansley interested in his whereabouts?'

'That,' Stevens replied, 'is not something Charnley discussed with me.'

'And Charles Crane?'

'That's the interesting thing. He asked me what I knew about Crane. Now it could have been he already knew you were acting in my corner over the Penry assault, had made the matrimonial connection — both you and Charles Crane had been married to Sandra — and was curious about the . . . coincidental connection? I don't know.' He paused. 'But I don't think it was that.'

'What do you think it was?'

'I'm not sure,' Stevens said slowly. 'But let me put it like this. Coppers don't offer information to the press — not unless they're fishing for something. Information, usually. And the kind of information they want, well, it normally becomes apparent, even obvious. With Charnley, I didn't have the slightest idea what he was after.'

Eric frowned. 'I don't understand.'

'Neither do I. He fished around, tried to find out what I knew about Crane, as though merely finding the bloody corpse gave me some kind of inside information about the man's background! But he didn't tell me anything; he was pumping me, but he gave me nothing. And how can you give answers when you don't really know what the hell the questions are?'

'It all seems pretty vague.'

Stevens picked up the spoon from his saucer and tapped it gently against the rim of the cup. 'Not entirely. If there was one thing that came across in the conversation, after the earlier cat-and-mouse business with me, it was that our friend Charnley was nervous about something.'

'About what?'

'Can't say. But it has something to do with Crane, I guess. But not so much as to why he was murdered, or by whom. More, it was to do with Crane's background.'

'So what is it you want from me?'

Stevens hesitated, watching Eric carefully. 'When I brought Mrs Crane to you today I had a chance to say a few things, ask a few questions.'

'And?'

'You've met her husband's partner.'

'Peter Stonier.'

'He reckoned Crane was pretty busy — outside the business.'

Eric hesitated, considering. There seemed little point in not telling the journalist since he would seem to have prised some information from Sandra already. Briefly, he told Stevens what he had learned from Stonier at Tiverton.

The reporter pursed his lips. 'Based in York, wandering around Teesside, Newcastle, Manchester. Interesting.'

'And shady, it would seem.'

'Airports.'

'What?'

'International airport at Manchester; links with Europe at both Newcastle and Teesside. And shady business.'

'So?'

'Teesside,' Stevens said slowly, 'was flushed out in 1979 as a drug centre. Same year, Manchester got hauled over, and a drug connection broken. Just a little while before our friend Lansley was hauled in and put away. The deal? For a tax evasion charge and nothing more, he shopped the drug connections?'

Eric considered the situation; it accorded with some of the admissions, hinted though they might have been, from Lansley at La Canebière. 'All right, but it's all a bit tenuous. What is it you want from me?'

'Let's put it like this,' Stevens said, leaning forward confidentially. 'You will have the forces of the newspaper syndicate marshalled behind you to find a link between Lansley and Sheridan Enterprises, Inc. And me — I'll have any admission you can wring out of the old bastard about a possible connection between Crane and Lansley.'

'But if such a connection is established,' Eric asked, 'where will that lead you?'

'Maybe,' the reporter replied cheerfully, 'to the reason why he was murdered — and maybe the name of the killer himself. And believe me, that's better than a badgerbaiting byline!'

* * *

Thin, low-lying cloud obscured the sun, leaving the narrow alleys shadowed in a pale, luminescent, unreal light. The atmosphere was humid, the traffic badtempered, and although the windows were closed to the noise and the heat and the wide ceiling fan moved regularly with a delicate sussurating sound, the big man sitting behind the desk in the narrow, dim room was sweating profusely.

Halliday Arthur Lansley looked different in these surroundings, in complete contrast to the *Alouette.* His grey suit, lightweight and well cut, removed some of the sagging paunchiness that had been so apparent on the yacht, and the air of Pickwickian contentedness had disappeared, to be replaced by a sharp, business-like attitude in which the charm had gone from his mouth and iron was apparent under the fatness of his cheeks. Lansley was still a man not to be trifled with, Eric thought, but next moment the man glanced up, and smiled, and the insincere warmth was back.

Lansley tugged out a spotless white handkerchief and applied it — gingerly to his sweating neck. 'I am surprised you insisted we met here, in my little backroom office, rather than down in the cool of the *Alouette,* Mr Ward.'

'I wanted this clearly to be understood as a business meeting,' Eric replied shortly.

'Most *positive* of you,' Lansley said and smiled again, injecting a hint of sadness into the grimace. 'And you have indeed been busy.'

'The decision of Mr Justice Stepford was communicated to you, I imagine.'

'I heard about it, yes. It did not surprise me. This—' he tapped the papers on his desk — 'does take me by surprise. Why have you bothered to be so *energetic*?'

'The Sheridan company will appeal.'

'If they are not persuaded otherwise?'

'That's right.'

'And why, pray, should I even attempt to persuade them?'

'Because they'll lose.'

Lansley put his head back, gazed thoughtfully at the slow gyrations of the fan above his head, and sighed. 'I think that is . . . how would you say . . . a moot point?'

'They'll lose, Mr Lansley, because I'll be able to show, on the basis of those papers, that the original transaction, and the defence raised by Sheridan Enterprises, is tainted with fraud.'

The innocent, china-blue eyes were fixed on Eric with a sudden sharp intensity. 'What do you suggest there is, in these papers you've brought to me, that indicates fraud?'

Eric leaned forward. 'Sheridan Enterprises, Inc. is an American based company, with American shareholders. One of the major investors in the stock is a company called Sun Station Holdings, Inc.'

'Such a charming name.'

'It is active in a small way in automobile repairs, but that's merely a cosmetic for a much larger operation as a holding company. It has an interlocking directorate with five other companies, in the States and Europe, but the most interesting fact that emerges is that in each case a considerable stock is held by a certain offshore dealing called Antibes International.'

'It conjures up pleasant vistas, does it not?'

'You own Antibes International. The papers prove it.'

'Yes,' Lansley murmured. 'Just exactly where did you get this information?'

'Let's say I've recently made connections,' Eric replied grimly.

'All right, on the assumption that what you say is correct, why are you presuming to suggest that you are, by holding these papers, able to hold the proverbial gun at my head? In the matter of Sheridan Enterprises, of course.'

Eric nodded. 'I think I'll be able to prove to the satisfaction of the English court that since you effectively hold a significant stake in Sheridan Enterprises, through the intermediate directorships, front men, and holding companies, and that you held such interests at the time of the sale of El Centro to Sheridan Enterprises, you were in effect selling to yourself.'

'Not entirely true, and you as a lawyer should appreciate that,' Lansley demurred. 'The company has a separate legal existence from its shareholders.'

'Granted, but when you transferred those holdings you already knew about the equity given to Morcomb Estates; the company will be *deemed* to have known the necessity for registration under Mexican law; your knowledge will be imputed to the company in which you hold shares; and the fact that you are now attempting to deny the validity of those shares equities—'

'It's the company denying it, dear boy, not I—'

'—the whole series of transactions is tainted with fraud, any attempt by Sheridan to overturn the decision of Mr Justice Stepford will be met by such an allegation, and the evidence of fraud will certainly prevent Sheridan from succeeding on the appeal.'

'Sheridan Enterprises could nevertheless continue,' Lansley suggested mischievously, 'bearing in mind the costs that Morcomb Estates might incur.'

'If I can prove fraud,' Eric promised, 'there could even be a criminal prosecution. That would bring you back to England, Mr Lansley.'

'A consummation devoutly *not* to be wished,' Lansley said, with a sigh. He leaned back in his chair, wiped his handkerchief over his pudgy cheeks and stared at Eric. 'All right, young man, I'll do what I can. Of all the arguments you've raised, the last is perhaps the most cogent. I would have advised the Board to fight, but . . . I will, even so, congratulate you on the efficacy of your contacts. I would never have believed it possible for this information —' and he placed his hands on the documentation in front of him — 'to be winkled out in such a quick time.'

'So you'll drop the appeal?'

'I will *advise* the Board, through my acquaintances among the directors, that persistence would be pointless . . . Ahh . . . quite stimulating, I consider. May I offer you a drink, now that our business is at an end?'

'No, thank you.'

'Of course, your care for your health. You won't mind if I, equally, look to mine. Whisky, I find, helps the circulation.' He produced a glass from the drawer, a bottle of malt whisky from the cupboard behind him, and poured himself a drink. He sipped it appreciatively. 'Cheers, and continued good health. You . . . ah . . . you have no information to impart to me with regard to the . . . ah . . . matter I discussed with you last time?'

'The man called Bartlett?'

'The same.'

'No.'

'You've had no report of his being on Tyneside?' The china-blue eyes were suddenly hooded. 'You've not heard anything of his . . . activities?'

'I have made some inquiries,' Eric replied reluctantly. 'And I've learned the kind of man he is. I'm told that he's violent and dangerous—'

'Indeed,' Lansley breathed.

' — and that he was recently released from prison. Moreover I am told he had worked for you—'

'Only intermittently, my dear fellow,' Lansley protested.

' — supplying you with muscle.'

'Well, let's say,' Lansley murmured with a secretive smile, 'that he was never employable in any intellectual league.'

'What about Crane?'

The china-blue eyes were hooded again. 'Who?'

'Charles Crane.'

'Ahh.' Lansley was silent for a little while, staring in owlish fascination at the glass of whisky in his hand. 'The name,' he said at last, 'has a familiar ring. Did I not hear recently from friends in the north of England that the body of a man called Crane has been discovered in some remote spot in Northumberland?'

'Rothbury Crags.'

'Beautiful spot.'

Eric had the impression that Lansley was teasing him, dangling him on the end of a string. Sharply he asked, 'Did he work for you?'

'Crane? Why do you ask?' Before Eric could reply, the big man went on slyly, 'Is it because of the marital coincidence?'

Eric sat still. 'How did you know about that?'

'My dear boy,' Lansley said soothingly, 'I've *told* you, I still have some friends in the North-East. Can you imagine the gossip not breaking forth, once it was discovered that Mrs Crane was formerly married to a policeman turned solicitor? I imagine *everyone* in the North-East knows about it now.'

Doggedly Eric said, 'You didn't answer my question.'

'Nor you mine. Why do you want to know whether I employed Crane? What makes you think I *might* have?'

'There's some evidence that Crane was involved in shady dealings. He had a carpet business in York; he travelled more than he needed to; his trips took him to towns which were known to have housed drug connections—'

'Ah, that old story again!'

'And if you talk about the *coincidence* of my ex-wife marrying Crane, what about the other coincidence: that he was chasing around these airports; that the drug rings were exposed; that you took a light gaol sentence; that Crane disappeared and was murdered?'

'If there is anything coincidental there,' Lansley said silkily, 'I fail to see it. And certainly, I see no possible connection, no possible inference you can draw between my activities and the death of Charles Crane.'

'*Did* you employ him?'

'In my heyday,' Lansley waved his pudgy hand airily, 'I employed many people, in various capacities, in various activities. But whatever I employed them as, they all had one thing in common.'

'And that was?'

'Greed. Was Mr Crane greedy, Mr Ward?'

'He was murdered.'

'Most greedy people manage to escape that fate,' Lansley said, smiling wickedly, 'but I concede the point; some don't.' He watched Eric warily for a few moments, summing him up, and then his smile grew broader, charming. He nodded. 'I tell you, Mr Ward — may I call you Eric? I *like* you. This matter of Sheridan Enterprises, for instance — I tell you frankly, it's only rarely that I've been bested in business matters like that. True, a few years ago, when I was more active, maybe I'd have taken you apart . . . but only maybe. Because where I've always been a wriggler, you're different. The good guys don't always win in the end, but I have a feeling about you. I'm old enough to be your father; you're the kind of son I would like to have had.'

Eric grinned. 'You're a liar.' He was amused, in spite of himself. 'You'd have wanted someone who was twice the rogue you are.'

'Have been,' Lansley corrected. 'All right, you're probably right. But you must look at my position, here in France. I sit here, alone—'

Eric raised his eyebrows. 'The yacht—?'

'Intellectually alone,' Lansley said, conceding the point. 'No longer *active,* in the business sense. In the *living* sense at all, I consider sometimes. But I know what goes on back in England, back in the North, and it interests me. I'm a distant observer of a faraway scene, and I'm aware of the jockeying, the manoeuvring, the wheeling, dealing, the *chicanery* . . .'

'You were part of it.'

'No longer.'

'But, even from a distance . . .'

'Yes. I know its heart.'

'Crane?'

Halliday Arthur Lansley squinted at the ceiling, inspected his whisky glass, scratched at the thin, red, bristling hairs on his head and pretended to look wise; he succeeded in only appearing careful. 'No. I wouldn't want to talk about Crane. But I will talk about other things. You have a good contact: the man who got you your information about my holdings. A newspaperman?'

Eric hesitated. 'Yes.'

'Then maybe I should give you a piece of advice.'

'Such as?'

'Cultivate him.'

'For what purpose?'

Lansley smiled, and touched the patchy skin on his cheek with a tentative finger. 'To find buried gold, perhaps? Let me put it like this, Mr Ward: this story of drugs, it is so old hat. Do you really believe the police would have settled for so little with me if they had possessed a case of any consequence against me? Tell your friend, your contact, to forget the drugs angle and look elsewhere.'

'In what direction?'

'Ah, now come, Mr Ward, you don't expect me to give all my little secrets away for nothing?' He spread his hands on the desk in front of him and contemplated them, smiling wryly to himself. 'I have already told you more than I should have done — but that's because I *like* you. But more . . . well, I'm not sure. I fear I sound coy, but one has to protect oneself. You do recall, however, that I told you at our last meeting I had been . . . involved with projects equally as exciting, in the old days.'

Eric nodded. 'You mentioned illegal immigrants, yes.'

'Indeed . . . The populations of Leeds and Bradford owe much to me; I was helpful in creating a multi-racial community there.'

'At a profit.'

'A *considerable* profit.' Lansley chuckled. 'Nevertheless, it wasn't the *only* bit of smuggling I did.'

'What else, then?'

'That's for your friend, perhaps, to unearth. As I said, there's buried gold to be discovered, Mr Ward, if only your journalist contact can find the right divining rod.'

3

Eric had been left with vague feelings of dissatisfaction after the interview with Lansley. The man had always been regarded as a smooth business operator, and Eric now felt that he recognized, personally, the other side of the man's character — charm and an easy manipulation of others. The hints the fat man had dangled in front of Eric had been frustrating, but more to the point, Eric had been left with the feeling that he was being used. He had tried to explain it to Eddie Stevens, when they met later that week.

'What I can't quite put my finger on is *why* Lansley is behaving the way he is. I get the impression that he's sitting there safely in the south of France, watching, listening, taking no active part in what is, or has been, going on, and yet in some odd way, he's pulling strings, making people dance to his tunes, working us all like the conventional puppets, but in a theatre of his choosing.'

He had said the same thing to Anne, but she had thought his imaginings fanciful. 'After all,' she said, 'you've got more or less what you wanted from him. He's agreed to tell the Board of Sheridan to back off on the appeal — and I've already heard, incidentally, that they want another meeting with our representatives soon, to *negotiate,* as they put it. So your trips to Marseilles haven't been wasted, it looks as though our investment is safe and we'll win the battle against Sheridan Enterprises, Inc. and it seems to me that it doesn't matter a damn whether Lansley has some nefarious reasons of his own for being so helpful to us.'

But it did matter to Eric. He didn't like the prickly, uneasy feeling that somewhere he was missing something, that Lansley was manipulating him for reasons he did not understand, and that all that had happened was somehow part of a wider, more dubious canvas. But it was not a matter he could talk out with Anne, for if he did so it would mean discussing with her the death of Charles Crane and that was something he knew might cause tensions to arise between them. Anne was still touchy about the reappearance of Sandra in his life; she felt he was wrong to help his ex-wife, and there was no reason why he should pursue the professional relationship with her. And in a sense she was right. His objective now should be merely to undertake the paperwork necessary for her to make the insurance claim with regard to her dead husband. He had that in hand. The insurance company would not prove difficult once the inquest formalities had been completed. Thereafter, Sandra could collect her money and run, establish her new life with her boyfriend, and there was no necessity for Eric to ever see her again.

And no necessity to get involved with any investigations into the death of Charles Crane.

Nevertheless, something disturbed him, a slow dragging at the back of his mind, a turgid snake of suspicion that at some point he was missing something that was important. He continued with his work at the office, prepared a few briefs for counsel on tax and conveyancing matters, entered three appearances in court and attended the first negotiations with Sheridan Enterprises in an advisory capacity at Anne's request. But he remained edgy. He wondered several times how Stevens was getting on with his own inquiries; he thought about Sandra, and how she would establish her new life with the mystery of her husband's death in the background; and he wondered about what Halliday Arthur Lansley was playing at.

Late the following week, on an impulse, Eric rang the Tiverton number of Peter Stonier, Charles Crane's ex-partner. There was no reply — indeed, the tone told him that the phone had been disconnected. During the next two days further inquiries led to a phone call with a businessman from Exeter who had had some dealings with Stonier.

'Packed in.'

'What?' Eric said.

'He's packed in. Gawn. Business was never too bright, and if you ask me, old Stonier, he was never too good at the game anyway. Contracts he had with me, I tell you, I did pretty well out of them. He could never have made much profit, believe me.'

'And now he's closed down?'

'Right. Don't surprise me. There's talk of converting the place into a hardware store. Crazy. That spot, just no good for business premises. Still, there's allus fools around, ain't it the truth?'

'Where has Stonier gone?'

'Can't say. Didn't noise it around. Just hope he makes a better fist of it next time, if there is a next time.' The businessman paused. 'People who might be able to tell you are Connolly's, though: they run a taxi business here in town and they had a maintenance contract with Stonier. They was pretty friendly, too, I think. Try them.'

Eric did. It was unproductive, and vaguely unsatisfactory. Connolly was significantly unhelpful; none of the drivers could help; they knew Stonier only vaguely; they were aware his business had closed down, but they had no idea where he had gone. And yet there was a defensiveness about the man's tone that suggested to Eric he knew more than he was saying.

It was nothing he could discuss with Anne.

* * *

Eddie Stevens was enjoying the luxury of being allowed freedom from the normal hack work he was involved in so that he could concentrate on the Halliday Arthur Lansley story. He had found Eric Ward's account of his conversation with the ex-financier in Marseilles interesting, but had not been entirely convinced by it. Nevertheless, though he still felt there was mileage in the drugs connection, and the police interest through Charnley in Crane's murder, there was no connecting link he could see, and Lansley's heavy hints led him to pursue other lines of inquiry.

Eric's confided feeling that he felt Lansley was somehow manipulating them cut no ice with Eddie Stevens. 'No, forget it. You got to understand, Mr Ward, people like Lansley, they get to like the limelight, they get to like the feeling of being regarded as important. All right, he's got quite a lifestyle, but he's still *missing* something — and that's the fact of being centre stage. He can't *be* centre stage any more, but he wants the kind of interest that will make him *feel* centre stage. You gave it to him. Believe me, the idea he's playing us is ridiculous. He doesn't care too much about what I'm digging into — and what's he told you, after all? Only to do what I'm doing anyway. No, believe me, I'm a good judge of crooked natures — after all, I've dealt with more than a few editors in my time! Believe me, he's no spider in a web: I know it, and I'm rarely wrong.'

In a matter of days, he was wondering whether this was an occasion when he had been wrong.

He had the confidence, when the Fleet Street barons suggested he should come to London, to take the morning flight from Newcastle Airport and charge it to expenses.

The conference he had with two senior editors in the newspaper syndicate and one of the directors was a heady experience as far as Eddie was concerned, and they seemed interested in what he had to say. The point he was stressing was that there was still mileage in the Lansley story; the man was still active in fraud as Eric Ward could show; that Lansley and Superintendent Chamley had now as good as admitted a cover-up in the drugs connection; and further probing by Eddie Stevens might yet uncover something sensational.

The barons seemed inclined to agree, and Eddie was then flattered to hear their suggestion that he should spend the afternoon with Tony Preston. It was a suggestion he quickly acceded to even though he was given no information regarding what the interview might bring about. Preston had a regular byline in one of the prestige Sundays, and was known for his work in London's greyer areas as far as crime was concerned. There seemed to be a hint behind the suggestion that to work along with Preston might be advantageous.

Preston met him at the door of his flat in Chelsea. The reporter was tall, thin, with sharp blue eyes and an ascetic face. He had heavy lids that tended to droop casually when he felt himself being observed, like a cat curling in upon itself before the claws emerged and the hairs rose. He invited Eddie into the flat, offered him a gin and tonic, sprawled in a chair with one long, elegant leg draped over the arm, and smiled in friendly fashion.

'I got a call suggesting a meeting between us would be advantageous.' He paused, choosing his words carefully. 'I'm not sure how I can help, if at all, but it might be useful if you were to sketch in some background for me.'

'I'm getting background on Halliday Arthur Lansley.'

'Old stuff.'

The disparagement raised Eddie's hackles momentarily. 'That's what a lot of people have been saying, but I've got the ear of the front office!'

The eyes were hooded swiftly, and Preston smiled. 'Yes, so it would seem. Hence this meeting. All right, what are you digging into?'

Eddie explained, telling Preston about the drug connection at the northern cities, the delivery systems through northern airports, and Eric Ward's account of Lansley's admissions. It was the last fact that raised Preston's interest visibly. He leaned forward. 'Lansley *admitted* this to Ward?'

'He did.'

'I wonder why?'

Eddie brushed the remark aside. He rushed on to talk about the fraud he had managed to dig out with the newspaper researchers' help, and the manner in which Lansley had swiftly capitulated to Eric Ward over the Sheridan situation. Preston regarded him thoughtfully for a while as he continued speaking, then he rose and poured himself another gin and tonic, and freshened Eddie's own drink.

'But I'm not yet quite clear what additional slants you might be able to give me,' Eddie said at last.

'Neither am I, dear boy,' Preston said casually, 'but it's always a good idea to have minds meeting, you know what I mean? Before we go any further, however, maybe I ought to suggest that . . . well, if we are to work together, maybe we should reach byline agreement.'

'A joint article, you mean?' Eddie was cautious. 'I'm not sure what you have, so . . .'

'I'm not quite sure, either,' Preston said smoothly, 'but I got the impression from the office that you have something else you're following up too.'

'The murder of Charles Crane.'

Preston flickered a quick glance over Eddie Stevens. 'Now that is more interesting than the Lansley stuff you give me so far. Did . . . did this Mr Ward raise Crane's name with Lansley?'

'Yes.'

'The result?'

'Noncommittal. He wouldn't talk about him. But he did give Ward a hint that he should be asking me to look elsewhere than into drug connections.'

'Indeed,' Preston breathed. 'Now that is interesting. What is the old fox up to?'

'I don't understand,' Eddie said uncertainly.

Tony Preston regarded him thoughtfully for several seconds and gently stroked the arm of the chair in which he was sitting. He smiled thinly, his eyes hooded once more. 'Well, let's put it like this. A man like Lansley, he doesn't give away information unless he gets something out of it.'

'Ward had him cornered.'

'Not very tightly.'

'Even so—'

'Even so, maybe I should tell you a little more about why the front office think we should talk together. A few years ago I was also chasing a Lansley story.'

'I never read—'

'I know, you'll have followed all published sources, but the fact is, my story was never published, because it was never completed. I don't like that happening; I feel dissatisfied if I spend months on something and it comes to nothing. The more so when I know there was something really there.' He put down his glass, rose and apologized for leaving the room for a moment. A few minutes later he was back with a small notebook. 'Tools of the trade,' he said, smiling.

'You've got information there about your Lansley investigation some time back?'

'Just let me refresh my memory a moment,' Preston said, and scanned the pages quickly, nodding to himself. Then he looked up, smiled brilliantly at Eddie and nodded. 'Not drugs,' he confided.

'But—'

'Lansley told Ward to forget the drugs. He was right.'

'You'll have to explain,' Eddie said, somewhat surly. He was becoming irritated by Preston's air of superiority.

'I got interested in Lansley some years ago,' Preston explained, 'as a criminal phenomenon. You see, he had his fingers in so many pies. I know it's common enough for criminals to diversify, but obviously it's not all that common for a man to range so widely over the field of so many legitimate and illegitimate enterprises. Yes, Lansley was into drugs for a while, but he was also into illegal immigrants, offshore companies, fraudulent trading, banking, travel agencies, you name it, he was there.'

'But you were interested in one operation In particular?'

'I was,' Preston said, nodding. 'Diamonds.'

Eddie stared at him, thinking. 'Eric Ward told me Lansley talked of buried gold.'

Preston smiled thinly. 'Figurative speech. But I wonder why he's been so cooperative . . . ? Anyway, the facts were that while I was in Amsterdam in the late 'seventies I was looking into the matter of shipments and thefts of industrial diamonds. It was a well-organized operation: the controller was known as Le Cochon — mainly because of his rather corpulent bulk.'

'Lansley?'

Preston shook his head. 'No, no, Le Cochon was a Dutchman. He's dead now. In fact, most of those involved seem to be dead now. Except Bartlett, of course.'

'Bartlett?'

Preston's glance slid thoughtfully over Eddie. 'That's right. You've heard of him?'

'No matter, go on.'

Preston hesitated, then went on. 'Anyway, I was tracing links but as I reached them, so they folded. The West Germans were cracking down at that time; the Sureté and Interpol were very active, and each time I seemed to be reaching a good story, so the operation closed down. Le Cochon's empire was dwindling swiftly, he was going out of business, and I guessed all I'd get in the end was a book, maybe, rather than a news series you know the sort of thing: *Inside Story of a Criminal Empire.*'

'And what happened?'

'Well, I struck lucky. Le Cochon was getting pretty desperate: his avenues were closing and he got less careful about the people he dealt with. And when his British runners fell out, he turned to someone you're interested in: Halliday Arthur Lansley.'

'Lansley ran a British diamond connection?'

'Precisely. To my eternal discredit, I kept the information to myself.' Preston smiled disarmingly. 'In other words, I kept my head down, needled out information, but told the police nothing. That was a mistake.'

'Why?'

'Politicians, like public servants, can be peculiarly vindictive. It's something to do with over-enlarged sensitivity glands. You see, I was all set to bring my story to a conclusion when I discovered something interesting. The police were interested, actively, in Lansley.'

'In regard to the diamond smuggling?'

Preston gave a brilliant smile. 'Not at all. Lansley is a clever man. It's true he had a hand in drug smuggling, but it was of such a nature that his personal involvement was minimal, and he could never actually have anything *proved* against him. But he *was* heavily into an operation which involved a delivery and distribution system for smuggled industrial diamonds. Le Cochon, raised the supplies in Europe; Lansley took them and "laundered" them in England through a network of agents in the North. But the police, they didn't have a clue he was so operating. They were obsessed with his drugs involvement. I think, now, that Lansley deliberately encouraged that.'

'You mean he used the drugs thing as a *front*.' Eddie asked unbelievingly.

'Not so dangerous as you might suppose,' Preston said. 'He could never get *nailed* for it; but if pressure ever came on him he could bargain his way out with information about drug connections.'

'Which is precisely what he did, when the axe fell.'

‘That’s right.’ Preston extracted a Balkan Sobranie from a gold cigarette case. He lit the cigarette thoughtfully and with care, his hooded eyes squinting slightly against the smoke as it rose. ‘Meanwhile, when the axe *did* fall I felt I was laughing all the way to the bank. Because I had the makings of another story: not only Lansley’s involvement in the industrial diamonds thing, but of the way he had fooled the police, even to the end. In other words—’

‘Your story would have been about police incompetence.’

‘Precisely. That’s why it was never published.’

Eddie Stevens frowned. ‘Pressure?’

‘Of the highest kind. Fleet Street can be the most able and courageous of animals; it can also be the most cowardly, given the appropriate circumstances. Just at that time two of the syndicate journals had been clobbered by the Press Council and there had been three hefty settlements, out of court, for libel actions. There was also the McReady affair.’

‘The child killer?’

‘That was the man. The *Journal* was accused of withholding evidence from the police. The DPP was all set to put his heavy boots on. And then in I sail with my story about police incompetence and the way Lansley had fooled them all to get a light sentence.’

Eddie grunted. ‘You were told to kill the story.’

‘That’s it, in a nutshell. I protested, of course. But the deal had been made. No more DPP scare, if I held back on Lansley and the innocent boys in blue.’ He shrugged. ‘I too have to make a living.’

Eddie Stevens leaned back in his chair, puzzled. ‘What gets me, after what you’ve said, is why I’ve been told to talk to you. Surely, if they wouldn’t print then, why should they do so now?’

‘Police pressure released,’ Preston replied laconically.

‘But *why*?’

‘You already have the answer,’ Preston said, inspecting the end of his cigarette. ‘You told me Superintendent Charnley questioned you about this man Crane.’

'That's right, but Lansley would say nothing about—'

Preston shook his head, interrupting. 'Crane worked for Lansley, all right. I have his name in my notebook. He ran a distribution system — not terribly efficiently — in the North-East.'

'That still doesn't explain why the possibility of the diamond smuggling operation being published now—'

'Maybe there's the chance of another trade,' Preston explained smoothly. 'Diamond smuggling is one thing; murder is another. I turned the operation run by Lansley inside out, but the police never got the details — after all, they didn't want to know, even denied its existence. But now they've got a murder on their hands, and they are not quite so sensitive. The incompetence story is a dead one anyway, years old; they won't mind a mild exposure of that, if they learn more about Crane and his activities.'

'But why haven't the police come to you?'

'I don't know, exactly,' Preston said thoughtfully. 'I think it's because the editors never told them who raised the Lansley information at the time. And when they did approach the newspaper this time, they were given your name. I think that's probably because the front office think you're someone to whom things . . . happen.'

Eddie knew what he meant, and it made sense. He was involved; he was warm with the story. For Preston it would not have been the same: a dead story, a hundred stories in between.

'I'm still interested, however,' Preston said, watching him carefully, 'why Lansley is being so free with his, albeit veiled, information.'

Eddie shook his head irritably. 'I don't see that matters too much. I can understand how the police might now be wanting urgently to clear up the Crane murder, but Lansley is irrelevant, and I'm more interested—'

'In Donald Bartlett?' Preston smiled. 'You'll have to excuse me for a moment.'

When Preston returned a few minutes later he was carrying a portable tape-recorder, and several tapes. He sat silently for a while, looking through his notes and checking against the tapes. At last he looked up, and nodded. 'I've got the one I wanted.'

'What is it?'

Preston slipped the tape into the machine and leaned back. 'You're already aware that Bartlett worked for Lansley.'

'Lansley as good as admitted that. I'm also aware that Bartlett recently got out of gaol, after a couple of years for strong-arm stuff.'

'In the course of my peregrinations,' Preston said in a sententious tone, 'I pick up snippets of information which I store away, for use on a rainy day. I've never been really very interested in this man Bartlett: he seems to me to be a mindless thug with not too much upstairs. But violent, and dangerous. The knowledge he's on the streets again does not fill me with the belief he is a reformed character. Anyway, I was taping interviews with various old lags a year or so back and I got this. We were talking about prison conditions and in the course of conversation, this is what I picked up, and taped . . .'

The man had a heavy Birmingham accent, overscored with resignation, the weighted scars of a twenty-year prison career. *'You think like all the blokes who visit and talk about these things that you can fit ideas, and people, and characters into little boxes. Don't happen that way. One man, he'll do his porridge standin' on his head. Some fellers, they fit in great, like it was 'ome from 'ome, you know what I mean? But there's the other kind too, the ones who get broody stuck inside. What's the word . . . if they got an . . . obsession, yeah, that's it. They can take it hard.'*

'How do you mean?'

Eddie Stevens glanced at Preston, recognizing the man's smooth tone in the question. The tape went on:

'Well, a bloke with an obsession, he gets tied up inside his head; it's like he can't think of nuffin' else. They're the bad ones; believe me. I remember once, I had to get a move almost as soon as I was twinned up with one feller. You got to realize, I was never muscle, you know? The con was my game.' There was a pause, a whirring

sound as though the tape had been faulty, patched up, and then the man from Birmingham was speaking again. '*. . . in the Scrubs, and once he found out I was a con man things got definitely ropey. I mean, I wasn't popular with him, you know? He told me, kind of nasty like, that he'd worked with some of the best, and been conned by them too, and then I used to catch him starin' at me, like he wanted to take me apart and not bother puttin' me together again. That's what I was talkin' about, see? He had an obsession, and he lived with it all the time. He used to mutter sometimes about getting it worked out, getting things straight, getting even, and it was all goin' on inside his head, all the time. It began to get me down, so I asked for a move. I got it too, after he had a shout at me one night, over nuthin' too. He was a real bastard, that one; a real rough bastard . . .*'

The tape sputtered, let a whining note emerge and Preston leaned over and switched it off. Eddie stared at him, not understanding. 'So what was that all about?'

'It was about an obsession.'

'*That*, I understand.'

'More specifically, it was about one man's obsession. It's not on the tape, but it's here in my notes. And now you've reawakened my interest in the man, and what I had in my notes.'

'Which was?'

Preston leaned back, considered for a moment. 'joint byline?'

Eddie hesitated. He shrugged. 'All right.'

'The man's violent cellmate was the man who was recently released from prison. His obsession was that he was conned, and that he intended doing something about it.'

'And his name, of course—'

'Donald Bartlett. Shall we have another drink?'

* * *

Confidence tricks could be played upon all sorts of people, and by all sorts of people, even newspapermen.

Especially newspapermen, Eddie Stevens thought sourly as he sipped his brandy dry on the return flight to Newcastle. He had the feeling he had been conned by Tony Preston.

The man had quite a reputation in Fleet Street, but he had done very little by way of investigative reporting during the last two years. And just what had he given Eddie Stevens for a joint byline on this Lansley/Crane business? Very little, Eddie reckoned. A tape that said very little; notes that said very little; a bit of guesswork but no facts of any note. And no real *links*, dammit, no real links.

Besides, like so many other people around, maybe including himself, Preston was obsessed with Lansley. Yet where did Lansley fit into anything, nowadays? Ward and Preston were both edgy about his motives, but Eddie knew that was rubbish. The man wanted attention, was playing a little game and nothing more. But Bartlett . . . and his nursing a grievance over a con . . .

Eddie took a taxi to his flat in Newcastle, paid it off at the door and took the lift up to his floor. He puzzled about what he had heard as the lift whined upwards; he was still puzzling over it when he settled with another brandy in his sitting-room. Eventually he reached for the phone and rang the number Eric Ward had given him.

'Ward? Eddie Stevens here.'

'You've not been in touch for a few days.'

'Busy. Chasing up this Crane thing . . . and Lansley.'

There was a short silence as though Eric Ward was unwilling to get dragged further into the affairs of the fraudulent financier and the dead man. At last, reluctantly, Ward said, 'So what have you got?'

'Not a great deal that makes much sense — except that I'm told I've been barking up wrong trees. It's diamonds, not drugs.'

'I don't understand.'

Stevens explained the story that Tony Preston had given to him and again there was a short silence. Finally Eric Ward asked, 'Why are you telling me all this?'

Stevens hesitated. 'I'm not sure. Maybe . . . maybe it's because I've got a particularly suspicious mind, and I don't like coincidences. There are too many coincidences around in all this, and . . . well, maybe I called you because I wanted to try to talk them out of my head, kick around a few ideas.'

'Such as?'

'Well, dammit, I get the feeling we're running around in some kind of tight circle, not getting anywhere — or at least not getting anywhere until we're allowed to. You know what I mean?'

'Manipulation,' Ward said quietly.

'Maybe, maybe, but don't give me the Lansley thing again. He's abroad, out of court, not involved. But what Preston was shoving at me was this character Bartlett. You told me Lansley was interested in Bartlett; we know now that Bartlett is nursing some kind of grievance, and he's out, and Lansley thinks he might be on Tyneside. And it's to do with a con. But what trick was pulled? Lansley's the trickster, the diamond smuggler, the drugs cover — if it was something to do with that why was Crane killed, and what's Bartlett doing, sniffing around Tyneside?'

'Mr Stevens, I'm not sure I want to know any longer. This kind of thing—'

'Yeah, I know,' Eddie interrupted him thoughtfully. 'But what's going on? Crane is a runner for Lansley; he gets knocked off; Lansley's muscleman sits in prison muttering about what he's going to do when he gets out; he slips back to Tyneside—'

'Mr Stevens—'

'All right, I know it, I'm rambling. I'm sorry to have bothered you. Good night, Mr Ward.'

Eddie put the phone back on its cradle and picked up his brandy. He sipped it, feeling its warmth against his tongue, and he sat there for a while, thinking. Somewhere in the train of events something was missing. People didn't always behave logically, they often had no pattern to their actions, but he had a feeling there was some kind of pattern in this chain of events, if only he could find the links. What were the isolated items that bothered him, that hummed around inside his skull like drowsy bees? Something Lansley had said: *'buried gold'* — Preston had laughed that off. Something he himself had said: *'coincidences'* — what was the biggest coincidence of all? Dammit, you could name *them*, not it!

He reached for his brandy again, found the glass empty, rose and spilled a small puddle of the liquid from the bottle into his glass. He put the glass down, stared unseeingly out of the window as he thought about coincidences, and the drowsy bees began to stir, move inside his skull, become more active, more alive as a pattern of thought and a pattern of behaviour began to take shape.

'Hell's flames!' Eddie Stevens said, and turned away in a surge of excitement from the window, heading again for the phone. The questions he now had to ask Ward—

The bell to his flat buzzed briefly, then again, more insistently. Eddie paused, looked at his watch, puzzled as to who might be calling on him, and reached for the phone. It was in his hand when the door bell buzzed again.

Eddie ignored it. He dialled Eric Ward's number. There was a short delay, and then Ward's voice came on.

'Mr Ward? This is Eddie Stevens again—'

The buzzer came again, insistently. Eddie swore.

'What's the matter?' Ward asked.

'I been thinking hard since I rang you a few minutes ago. About cons, and cover-ups, and manipulations and coincidences. Tell me—'

This time the buzzer would not be denied. A long, continuous droning sound filled the room as though the person outside was leaning on the buzzer. Eddie swore again. 'Look, Mr Ward, I'm sorry about this but I better call you back.' He slammed down the phone and angrily headed for the door. He flung it wide open. There was a man standing in the corridor. For a moment Eddie failed to recognize him.

Eddie grabbed for the door, tried to slam it in the man's face but he was too late. A heavy body blocked the doorway, a muscular shoulder preventing it from shutting. Eddie gasped, thrusting at the door but a vicious swinging kick struck him below the kneecap and he staggered backwards; the door was flung open again and a fist was driven into Eddie's groin. He collapsed, retching and breathless with pain as the agony reached up from his lower stomach.

As he lay there he heard the slamming of the door. He was lying on his side, gasping with pain and he saw the man's shoes, toecaps scuffed and dirty. He heard the voice he had last heard in the courtroom.

'Now, you bastard, time to get what you deserve!'

'Penry!' Eddie had time to gasp just the one word before the shoe swung at him, struck him in the armpit and then swung again. And again.

In a little while the rhythmic thudding in his brain slowed, and there was only a black silence.

CHAPTER 5

1

'And where do we now stand in the saga of Mrs Sandra Crane?' Anne asked.

She was sitting on the low wall at the back of the house, facing him. Behind her, Eric could see the sweep of the hills, dark in the bright morning sunlight. Anne's face was shadowed, her voice mocking, but he knew her well enough to realize there was an edge of seriousness in her tone. He smiled. 'The insurance company have agreed to pay up. I have the necessary papers. It's just a matter of her calling to collect them.'

'I'm surprised she hasn't already done so. She wouldn't want you to *post* them, of course — that would lose her the opportunity of seeing you again.'

'Jealousy never becomes a woman.'

'I'm just recognizing your tremendous attractiveness, darling.' She was grinning as she said it, but then she became serious, staring at him thoughtfully. 'You know she wants something from you, don't you?'

'My body?' he teased her.

'Huh! She had that years ago and—' Anne bit off the words, and then went on, 'But anyway, there's something she wants.'

'Settlement of her insurance claim.'

'No. She could have got that done by any lawyer in town. No, something else.'

'What, then?'

'I don't know. But I have a feeling . . . woman's intuition, if you like.'

'*Wife's* intuition,' he corrected her. 'Much more deadly.'

'You won't take me seriously.'

'Look, Anne,' he said patiently, 'let's just forget the whole thing. It's all but over anyway. As soon as she gets in touch with me I'll get the papers to her, she'll sign them and that will be that.'

'You shouldn't have ever got involved with her again in the first place.'

'I'm not *involved*.'

'You're worried, nevertheless.' She watched him carefully, the sunlight striking red-gold tints in her hair. 'And what about this Stevens thing? He was involved with her, wasn't he?'

Eric shook his head. 'You're drawing threads together where there's no connection. He was involved with her only in the sense that he was interested in discovering who killed her husband. The beating he took the other night had nothing to do with that. The man who attacked him is Penry, and he's back in police custody — now facing even more serious charges.'

'Stevens was badly hurt, wasn't he?'

'Eddie Stevens will recover,' Eric said, 'but not for a while. He's still under sedation, his jaw is wired, he can't speak, he has pelvic and chest injuries . . . all in all he's in a bit of a mess. Penry will really get the book thrown at him now, the stupid—'

'Why didn't you tell the police that Stevens called you only seconds before the beating?' Anne asked sharply.

'Because . . .' Eric hesitated, groping for the right words. 'Because it wasn't relevant.'

'It was about Sandra Crane, wasn't it?'

'How do I know? He didn't get around to telling me. The earlier call was all about Crane's death, and a man called Bartlett, and Lansley . . . but it was all so confused, and he was doing little more than thinking aloud.'

'But when he rang back . . .'

When he rang back, Eric thought, he had perhaps done his thinking, maybe wanted a few confirmations, but had probably already reached some tentative conclusions. And they involved Eric Ward.

'Well, you're well out of it,' Anne said and went into the house.

But he wasn't out of it. He did not want to discuss it with Anne, because she might have become alarmed, and also because anything to do with Sandra Crane was regarded by her with intense suspicion. More than that, there was the puzzle why the journalist had thought it *necessary* to speak to Eric; it was true that the beating Stevens had taken had nothing to do with the phone call, but Eric now felt an odd debt to the injured man. It was nothing he could explain to himself. But Stevens had had something important to say, and hadn't had the chance to say it before he was viciously beaten.

There was something else that had been bothering Eric, in addition. The talk of Bartlett on Tyneside was one thing; the information that Crane had been involved in the smuggling of industrial diamonds was another. But what really bothered Eric in a way he could not explain was the disappearance of Peter Stonier. Eric had put out some feelers through his contacts on Tyneside, and inquiry agents had been active in the West Country, but Stonier seemed to have vanished off the face of the earth.

Moreover, it was a source of irritation to him that he had not seen Sandra for several days, and when he had last spoken to her on the phone, regarding the insurance claim, she had been somewhat evasive regarding her address.

'I won't be able to contact you when the papers come through,' he'd complained.

'That's all right.' There had been an edge of nervousness in her voice. 'I'll ring in a couple of days. You can tell me then. The fact is, I'm looking for a place to stay: I'm with friends right now, but there's no point in giving you their address because in a day or so I'll probably be moving.'

'Sandra—'

'No, it's all right, I'll be in touch . . .'

It was all very unsatisfactory, and vaguely disturbing and now the papers had come through he felt edgy. He was unable to put aside Anne's comments, either: *she wants something from you.* Something she would not get from another solicitor. He thought over his meetings with Sandra Crane, and one in particular, and although he was left with a feeling of uneasiness, there was nothing he could really identify, nothing he could seize upon as special in their relationship.

On the Thursday morning the weather was thundery; as he made his way to the Crown Court Eric felt uncomfortable in the humidity. The air was heavy, shafts of sullen sunlight flickered through menacing cloud and he was aware of the old, familiar prickling behind his eyelids, presaging an uncomfortable period for him unless he took a dose of atropine. He did so in the privacy of the cloakroom, and then attended the hearing at which he was representing a local businessman in a tax matter. The courtroom was stifling, the judge bad-tempered and the proceedings appallingly slow. By the end of the afternoon Eric's shirt was sticking to his back and he felt irritable and tired. He decided he would not attempt the journey back to Sedleigh Hall and phoned Anne to tell her he would be staying at the flat. He made his way down to the Quayside, to check at the office if there had been any messages. There had been.

'Mrs Crane rang,' Lizzie explained, scratching at her garish punk locks, 'and when I told her you had received the papers she said she'd call in to sign them this evening.'

‘What time did she ring?’ Eric asked.

‘About half an hour ago. She said she’d be here before seven, if that was all right. I wasn’t sure . . .’

‘That’s all right, Lizzie. You get off home. I’ll stay here, and wait to see Mrs Crane.’

When he was alone in the office he stood in front of his window staring out over the river and the Quayside. A Norwegian freighter was getting ready to catch the tide at Tynemouth but it was the only craft in sight, and the Quayside was quiet, as though all activity had been dulled by the heavy, torpid clouds. He broke one of his rules as he stood there and took a small glass of whisky and water; he felt vaguely troubled, not at the thought that this meeting would probably be the last he would have with Sandra, but aware in some distant way that the attack upon Eddie Stevens had prevented something happening that could have been important to Eric Ward.

She came shortly after seven o’clock.

She was wearing a light-coloured dress and an anxious expression; her flecked eyes seemed unwilling to meet his, and there was a tension in her bearing that suggested she would welcome a swift end to the meeting. He motioned her to a chair; she sat on its edge, as though poised for flight, or argument.

‘I’m sorry to have kept you waiting.’

‘That’s all right,’ he said. ‘I was staying in Newcastle anyway . . . I’ve got the papers here, and they’re marked for your signature. Don’t date them; I’ll see to that.’ He handed the papers across to her. ‘You’d better read them before you sign.’

She scanned the sheets swiftly, her lips moving with the words, and he watched her, feeling the tension that lay between them, puzzlingly. Outside there was a low rumbling sound, distant thunder rolling in the electric air. ‘You’ve managed to find a place to stay permanently now?’ he asked.

‘What? Oh . . .’ She frowned, then shrugged dismissively. ‘Yes, that’s right, but not exactly permanent. The cheque—’

'Is here,' Eric said. He passed her the envelope. 'Now you've signed the release forms, it's all yours.'

'Thank you.'

'What'll you do with it?'

She stared at him blankly, and after a moment dropped her head, thrust the envelope into her handbag. 'Not sure, yet. We'll . . . we'll think about it, probably go away—'

'When you've only just found a place?' Eric asked, surprise straining his tone.

'It's not . . . permanent,' she said, and rose to leave. 'I . . . I ought to thank you now, Eric, for acting for me. It's been a bad time, and if I seem . . . disorientated, well . . . you must understand.' She fumbled awkwardly with her handbag, staring about her as though seeking some method of escape. 'And I'll need to pay you for your services. I could make out a cheque now—'

'I'll send you a bill, in a few days.'

Her green-flecked eyes widened slightly at the thought and she licked her lips nervously. 'No . . . I might be travelling. Better if I paid now.'

'I haven't prepared the bill.'

'No matter. I know I can trust you. I'll give you a blank cheque. After all, a solicitor, an ex-policeman, and an ex-husband all rolled up in one, if I can't trust you, who can I trust?' She managed a laugh but it had all the conviction of an uncertain witness.

Eric stared at her as she drew out the cheque-book, signed and dated a blank cheque and ripped it out. It tore at the corner and she glared at it with a helpless desperation before she handed it to him. He took it, wordlessly, and she stood up, held out her hand. 'Thank you, Eric, and goodbye. I won't bother you again.'

'No,' he said.

There was a long pause as she stared at him, and then she turned away, releasing his hand. He watched her leave the room, heard her clatter down the stairs and then he stood by his window, watching the Quayside. She emerged from his office, turned left and began to walk towards Dog Leap Stairs. Only then did he decide to follow her.

* * *

It proved to be easier than he had anticipated, but a longer job than he had expected. As he left the office she was still in sight; he took the precaution of hailing a taxi and with a brief explanation that he was a solicitor making inquiries found that the perspiring taxi-driver was not averse to a little excitement at the prospect ahead of him. So, as Eric walked some distance behind Sandra, up through Grey Street, the taxi managed to maintain a discreet distance behind him. When Sandra stopped at the green car parked at the top of Grey Street and unlocked it Eric waved the taxi forward, and got in. 'Here's where it starts, hey?' the taxi-driver said hopefully.

'Looks like.'

They left Newcastle by the North Road and the taxi-driver's skill was such that they kept well back in the fairly heavy traffic that filtered out of the city northwards. Sandra Crane drove carefully and unflamboyantly; it meant that Eric's driver was able to make use of caravans and holiday traffic as a screen for much of the way along the North Road.

At Alnwick, Sandra swung left to skirt the town, heading towards the valley of the Coquet. It was an area familiar to Eric, since he came this way often enough to reach Sedleigh Hall, and as the traffic thinned suddenly, making the chance of Sandra noticing she was being followed more likely, Eric tapped the driver on the shoulder.

'There's a three-mile run now if she stays on this main road; I know the back roads to the Coquet. If we turn left at the next junction, we can pick her up again in about two and a half miles. That's right . . . the junction up there.'

The driver obediently took the side road at the fork while Sandra drove on; Eric looked back to the fork and there was a dark blue Ford which had stopped at the junction. As he watched, the Ford driver obviously made up his mind and slid back to the main road. Eric suggested his driver speed up since the back roads were rather slower than the one which Sandra had taken. The driver was pleased to display his skill, and by the time they finally came back to the main road Sandra, Eric guessed, would be no more than half a mile ahead.

He was right. As they topped a rise, and the road fell away below them into a valley edged with hornbeam and flushed by rosebay willow herb, Eric caught sight of the blue Ford, pottering its way down to the valley floor, and on the winding road ahead, cutting into the steep slope below the quarry, he caught the glint of late sunlight on Sandra's windscreen. Eric told the driver to take it easy, keeping the Ford between them and Sandra, because the road would now lift into the hills above the Coquet, winding up towards Simonside and the Cheviot. As it happened, however, the Ford bumbled its way into a layby just as the road began to rise. Eric glanced at the car as they passed but its solitary occupant was leaning sideways, inspecting something. Next moment they were around the swing of the next bend and climbing.

The last of the sunshine had now gone and the clouds were heavy again above the Cheviot. The window of the taxi was open, but the breeze was not cool to Eric's cheek: it was warm and heavy under the threatening skyline. Below them to their left the Coquet wound dully, grey under the thundery sky, and a yellow haze seemed to fill the valley, a drifting summer torpidity, waiting for the storm that it presaged.

Over the skyline the road twisted and turned, sliding past rocky outcrops and slicing through scarred hillsides; heather thickened on the slopes above, providing cover for black grouse, and high above the hill itself Eric could see a hawk, motionless against the blackening sky. When the fork came up ahead of them the driver slowed, questioningly. Eric hesitated; the road ahead of them to the left would run down into Rothbury and he could see its surface light against the pinewood clump of afforestation. There was no car on that stretch. He waited for perhaps thirty seconds and then, as he heard the vague grumbling of a car behind them he instructed the taxi-driver to take the right fork.

It ran level for perhaps three hundred yards and then abruptly narrowed, meandering into a track that twisted deep-rutted through a scattering of Scots pine and thick undergrowth. As it began to descend Eric told the taxi-driver to stop. He got out of the taxi and asked the man what he owed him.

'You payin' me off here?' the man asked in surprise.

'That's right.'

The man stared about him, perplexed. 'But how'll you make it back?'

'I'll manage.' Eric paid the man what he asked, and then watched him reverse into the trees, turn and make his way back to the main road. Eric turned, and walked along the rutted track. In a few minutes his guess was proved right.

The smallholding would have met its agricultural end some years ago: the yard was overgrown, the stables tumbledown, and where chickens had scratched there was now a muddy expanse of weed, where the drainage had broken down. The house itself retained a defiantly solid appearance, however; its grey, stubborn stone and slated roof held back the elements still, and if its narrow windows seemed suspicious of the outside world the house itself was nevertheless beautifully set in the tiny dell, its back against the slope of the forested hill, and the tiny garden at the rear sheltered, a suntrap on better days. Whoever had tried to scratch a living here at one time had abandoned the idea in favour of holiday lettings, Eric guessed.

Holiday lettings . . . or short-term stays.

Some fifty yards away from the cottage, and among the trees above the parked car Sandra had driven here, Eric stood with his back against a tree and waited, watching the cottage. He thought of Eddie Stevens and Halliday Arthur Lansley and Charles Crane. And Sandra Crane. Coincidences, Stevens had said over the phone. Coincidences, and links . . . and logic. Scenes flickered through the mirrors of Eric's memory, and he puzzled about what exactly Eddie had wanted to ask him, and tell him. Above his head the sky grew darker, heavy storm clouds now obscuring the Cheviot, and the yellowish light crept into the glen, quietening the bird life, until the hush was complete except for the occasional crackling of twigs in the wood behind him. After a while even they stilled, as the storm gathered its strength and reached out for the valley.

Only when the first heavy drops came pattering through the trees and the wind began to lift, bringing the thrust of the storm through the long grass did Eric move. He had by then thought about the coincidences, and had decided it was time to confront Sandra Crane. He walked down as the first jagged flicker of electricity shattered the sultry air, and he tapped on the door of the grey-stone house in the glen.

* * *

Something happened to her face as she stared at him in utter surprise, one hand holding the door ajar, the other leaping involuntarily to her mouth. Her eyes flared, green-flecked, and for one moment, as the incomprehension gave way to a sudden panic, there was a hunted shadow deep in her glance. 'Eric!' she said loudly and stepped backward, away from the door, but her tone of voice suggested she was over the initial reaction, and getting control of herself.

He stepped over the threshold into a dark timbered room, furnished with elderly sagging chairs and settee, and a battered mahogany table in the far corner near the window, serving as a dining area. A fire in the hearth was already ablaze, and the room was warm; a newspaper lay discarded on the floor beside one of the armchairs. Sandra stooped above it, began to fold it in a haphazard manner. 'What on earth are you doing here?' she asked.

'I thought you might ask how I found my way,' Eric suggested.

'All right, how did you?' she said with a flash of defiance. 'I suppose you followed me.'

'That's right.'

'Why?'

'To get the answers to some questions.' He hesitated. 'They're questions I've been slow to raise, perhaps because I've been reluctant to face them.'

'What sort of questions?'

'Why you came to see me to help you; why you've recently been so secretive about your address; what you really wanted from me.'

She turned to face him; for the first time he noted how years of dissatisfaction had pulled like wires at the corners of her mouth, as though she resented what she had lost. A rocky childhood had made her tough and self-sufficient, that he knew; her selfishness had grown with womanhood but now there was more than that. 'What did I want?' she asked, with a hint of mockery edged with nervousness. 'I wanted your legal help.'

'More important,' he said slowly, 'you wanted my gullibility.'

There was a short silence as she stared at him, then she turned away, folding her arms across her chest in an oddly defensive gesture. 'I don't know what you mean.'

'You wanted a lawyer, yes; but you also wanted one who wouldn't ask too many questions, and one who, if he did begin to question things, could be turned aside, thrown off the track. I was chosen by you because of what we once were to each other, and because you could use the past to deflect me, confuse my thinking.'

'You're wrong, I—'

'First of all there was the coincidence — your arriving on my doorstep almost immediately the body of your husband was discovered, with a relationship already established with me, and then when I found nothing of your husband's whereabouts, a second discovery by the police, the ring which you were able to identify. Was it you who returned up there to plant it? Or did you put it there right at the beginning, when you buried him?'

Shock registered nakedly on her face now and she glared at him, anger and fear stripping away all pretence. 'You don't know what you're saying. I don't have to—'

'Where is he?' Eric asked quietly.

'Who?'

'Stonier.'

The silence grew around them. Outside, the wind had begun to rise and the menacing rumble of thunder was less distant, the storm growing closer and gathering above the valley in which Sandra had gone to ground. The yellowish light was reflected into the small room, brightened momentarily by the flicker of lightning. A board creaked in the house, the soft movement of weight, a shifting body. Then the door to Eric's right opened slowly, and he stepped into the room from the scullery.

'How did you know?' he asked in a dead voice.

'That you were here?' Eric gestured about him. 'The fire, the newspaper—'

'No. About me and Sandra.'

Eric stared at him. Peter Stonier was pale with tension and it robbed his skin of some of its tan. He was dressed in sweater and jeans and it removed some of his ruffled charm, making him seem older and more vulnerable. Anxiety moved deep in his bleached eyes, darkening them, murky fears staining their blueness, and Eric shook his head. 'I didn't. It was merely an educated guess. The kind I should have made some time ago, but Sandra used my . . . gullibility. The way you two met when I visited Tiverton; the way she insisted on coming down; the way, when I tried to suggest I was suspicious about you she diverted me, in the easiest manner possible — by playing on an old, dead relationship and suggesting she wanted to go to bed with me.'

Stonier glanced at her quickly, moistened his lips. 'Even so—'

'She'd already told me she had a lover, a man she wanted to marry. I met you; she never said you were the man though she did tell me you'd *fancied* her, when Crane "left". And then, when Crane's body is identified and I try to get in touch with you, no one seems to know where you are. You disappear as effectively as Charles Crane did. And suddenly, Sandra too is not available, can't be contacted. Just an educated guess, as I say, but even then I didn't raise it until someone else began to question the coincidences.'

'Who?'

'A journalist called Eddie Stevens. He rang me. I think now he'd begun to wonder about the background to Crane's murder; had suddenly asked about Sandra's appearance before me just after the body was found; begun to wonder if she came then to set me on the trail, to establish *bona fides* with regard to the insurance policy because she knew the body at Rothbury Crags was Crane's — *because she and her lover put it there.*'

Involuntarily, Sandra Crane moved closer to Peter Stonier. The man himself hesitated, edgy, not knowing what to say. He raised a placatory hand. 'You've got this all wrong, Ward. It just wasn't—'

'Explain how it *was*, then, Stonier,' Eric demanded. 'The way I see it, Charles Crane was an absent husband, chasing around on illicit deals for Halliday Arthur Lansley — yes, I know about that side of his activity! His absence gave you time, and Sandra the predilection, for an affair. But what went wrong? Did Crane find out? Or did you cook this plan up between you?'

The bleached blue eyes glared at Eric, shadowed by reluctant memories he tried to dispel by an angry shake of the head. 'I don't know what plan you're talking about, Ward.'

'The business you had going at York with Charles Crane was going bust, largely because he was more concerned with other activity. You must have guessed at the end that there was something odd about his travels; you and Sandra probably didn't want any involvement with the Lansley business, but there *was* an insurance policy lying in the background.'

Sandra's hand crept out tentatively, touching Stonier's arm. Her lips were pale with anxiety. 'Peter—'

'Be quiet,' he said with an authority that lacked conviction. 'He doesn't know what he's talking about — he's making wild guesses—'

'You'll both have thought about that insurance policy,' Eric continued coldly. 'If Crane was dead, the business could go to hell, you and Sandra would have a nest egg to start up with again once the money was claimed, and you could start a new life. But there was one problem: you would have to give things time to settle down. If Crane died violently the police would investigate; your relationship with Sandra would have to seem a thing of the past, if it ever came to light at all. You had to avoid suspicion settling on you . . . on either of you. So you hid the body of Charles Crane at Rothbury Crags.'

Sandra shivered. Stonier stood squarely, facing Eric, his face impassive, but his eyes shifting as though seeking escape.

'After that,' Eric went on, 'you and Sandra stayed apart as much as possible, while you waited for someone to find the corpse at the Crags. It took some time . . . but the moment the body was found, even before it was identified, Sandra came to see me, to ask me to find her husband. And when I asked her the obvious questions, she was frank: if he was dead, she wanted to claim on the insurance policy. I was disarmed by that frankness, but then, my gullibility was an important element in the success of your scheme.'

'You can't fix all this—'

Eric shook his head. 'I always felt your story about the signature on the lease was an unlikely one. There was something odd about the whole interview at Tiverton; I felt you were giving some kind of performance. You were frank enough, telling me you'd forged that signature, but you didn't forge it to pay off the debts; you forged it to maintain the illusion at that time that Crane was still alive! You needed the time — you *both* needed the time — to set the scene. And you got it.'

Sandra Crane gripped Stonier's arm hard. Her palpable nervousness suddenly seemed to give him strength, and as he turned to glance from her to Eric his confidence seeped back, his mouth tightening with resolve, his fists clenching. 'This is a load of rubbish, Ward, and we both know it. I've got reasons of my own for being here at this cottage; the fact that Sandra and I are lovers is nothing to do with that, or with you. You've done all you were required to do for us; you'll never be able to prove Sandra and I were lovers before Crane disappeared. In fact, what the hell can you prove? All you're doing is constructing some kind of wild scenario, indulging your own fantasies.' He paused, eyeing Eric carefully, and nodded. 'In fact, if you really believed what you're saying, would you be here at all? Why didn't you go to the police? Why walk into this crazy confrontation? If you really thought we were murderers would you have come here alone?'

Eric paused, looked at Sandra. 'Maybe it was because I still couldn't believe that Sandra could be mixed up in something as messy as this. When you've known someone, there are things you remember . . . but I guess much of it is wishful thinking, because you can't really get inside someone's head, or personality. I came for confirmation. I think—'

'I know,' Peter Stonier interrupted him, making a chopping gesture with his hand. 'I know you've no proof about anything you've been saying, and it's all just wild guesswork on your part. And that means neither Sandra nor I have any reason to stay here and listen to all this. Sandra's got what she's been waiting for. We can leave now.'

Sandra Crane glanced at Eric uncertainly. Much of the strength seemed to have drained from her as he had spoken; the confidence she had displayed ever since her return to Newcastle had become eroded, as though she was no longer capable of ordering her life in the manner she had planned. Eric's words had shaken her, and she needed reassurance. Eric wondered briefly whether she had indeed been involved in her husband's death at all, but next moment Peter Stonier was reaching out, taking her hand. 'We've got to go, Sandra.'

She gathered strength from his touch, sent a flickering glance towards Eric and then remarked, 'I don't know where we can—'

'*Sandra.* This man followed you. Others could equally do so. We must go, now.'

Numbly, uncertain, Eric stood aside as they walked towards the doorway. There was nothing he could do to stop them; Stonier had been right. He had no proof, but more, Sandra had perhaps been right in her own, earlier calculations. He did not have the will to interfere: all this was nothing to do with Eric Ward, it was all part of a life which she had entered and in which he had no place.

The door opened, and Stonier stood framed there, still holding Sandra's hand. He looked back, half smiling his growing contempt and confidence, and the thunder growled above him. Next moment he had stepped through the doorway with Sandra and Eric was alone in the house.

He waited a moment, looked around for a phone, for he would need to call for transport. There was no phone. He paused, walked to the doorway and then stood there, staring dumbly out to the small clearing where the green car was parked. The scene etched into his mind, raising other scenes, other visions in his brain. Peter Stonier stood under a darkening sky with his hand on the handle of the car door, against a backdrop of black woods. Sandra stood beside him, a little to one side, half covered by his body, seeking protection. They were both riveted by the sight of the other figure, standing some twenty yards away from them.

Stonier had been right: where Eric Ward had followed, so could someone else.

The man was angular in build, lantern-jawed, tense in his stance. He had black, springy hair, and a heavy body that gave the impression it was built for blind force. His mouth was stiff, announcing a dislike for the world, and his glance proclaimed his resentment of the treatment that world had afforded him. He was a dangerous animal, a man accustomed to reacting to instinct, and his instinct was rooted in violence. The fingers of his left hand were crooked in angry spasm; in his right hand he held a gun. Eric recognized the weapon: a .357 Magnum, the most powerful handgun in the world.

He stared again at the man's face. There was no sense of shock in him because recognizing the man, accepting the recognition as a fact, was like the playing again of a familiar worn piece of ancient film, images that were filed in his brain yet which had not been brought forward until now. There was the faint memory of a snapshot to which he had paid little attention when Lansley had shown it to him: a man in rough seaman's clothing against a background of North Shields cranes. There was the brief, dimly seen vignette of the day Sandra had first visited his office and had walked away on the Quayside, to be followed by a man with black, springy hair. And there had been the day he had taken Sandra to Exeter when he had seen the same man at Central Station, and again in an altercation at the taxi-rank in Exeter. Why had Eric not fitted the images together? Faces out of context, a mind on something else, failure to concentrate and fit an image to another.

This man had followed Sandra on the Quayside; he had tried to follow her and Eric in Exeter and failed; and now there was another image in Eric's brain: a blue Ford car bumbling along behind him, then reluctant to be sandwiched between the cars used by Sandra and Eric . . . an uncertainty at a fork in the road . . . Eric stood riveted, vision clouded as he stared at the three people in the frozen tableau in front of him, understanding at last, yet not quite understanding.

The handgun wavered slightly, then described a slow, menacing arc in Eric's direction. The stiff mouth twisted, and when he spoke the man's voice was low, and cold. 'You . . . you better step over here with these two.'

Eric hesitated. While he had walked down the track earlier the blue Ford had turned in, been parked, and the man with the gun had followed Eric down the track. He had waited behind him, as Eric stood thinking things out — the crackling twigs in the forest should have warned him — and now, having successfully traced the people he was seeking, the man felt confident, alert and satisfied. Eric stared at the gun, considering: over-confidence could result in over-reaction.

The man was watching him with hard, calculating eyes. They held a professionalism that Eric recognized: this man had killed in the past, knew what it was like to kill. There would be no compunction in acting. if action was called for.

'I said step over here, where I can see you properly. I won't say it again.'

Eric moved carefully and slowly, saying nothing. He held his hands in a neutral position, slightly raised, palms outwards.

Stonier and Sandra were rigid, glaring at the man with the gun in stunned fascination. They paid no attention to Eric, as he joined them.

He took up a position within the range of the gun, slightly to one side of the stiff figures of Peter Stonier and Sandra Crane, and he stared at the man in the dark sweater and black trousers.

'You're Donald Bartlett,' he said quietly.

The man with the gun looked him over coldly, dismissively. 'And you finally led me where I wanted to be,' he replied. His grey eyes flickered back to Peter Stonier. 'Time for a reckoning, friend,' he grated.

'Bartlett,' Stonier said quickly, nervously, 'I got nothing you could want.'

'No?' The handgun moved, its deadly muzzle lifting slightly. 'You got a *lot* I want, a lot I mean to get. I had plenty of time to think about it while I was inside, and I had it worked out. The trouble was, finding you. But she was careful . . . and this man Ward was in the way . . . but I finally got to you.'

Eric cleared his throat and shifted from one foot to another. 'I heard about your obsession, Bartlett.'

The grey eyes were suddenly sharper as they fixed on Eric, but the gun remained trained on Peter Stonier. 'Is that so? I doubt it.'

'Diamonds.'

'Well, well, well,' Bartlett said softly. 'So you know about what was going on, after all.'

'I know that Stonier's partner, Charles Crane, was a courier for Halliday Lansley, and I know that you provided strong-arm assistance when it was needed. But that's all over, and there's no need to wave that bloody gun—'

'There's every reason, *Mister* Ward,' Bartlett snapped, and anger boiled into his tone. 'I said, I had time to think while I was in prison. You don't know the bloody story! The shipment—'

'Bartlett,' Stonier said with a hint of desperation, 'I swear—'

'There was a shipment of industrial diamonds coming in at Manchester. I was working for Lansley, but he was on the slide. He was under all sorts of pressures, his source in Amsterdam was on the skids as well, and I knew it was only a matter of time before Lansley was for the high jump. So I was looking for a way of easing myself out. Then Lansley told me about this shipment; said it was important to him; told me he didn't trust his courier, Crane. He sent me over to Manchester Airport to make sure the courier did as he was supposed to do. And when he didn't, I knew my chance had come.'

Stonier was sweating in the electric, humid air. He shook his head. 'Bartlett, you got it wrong. It's not the way you think it was.'

'I got it right, believe me,' Bartlett said sourly. 'Crane made the pick-up as directed, but instead of driving to Leeds he headed for Newcastle There was a house in Jesmond; he parked the car in the garage, and it's then that I caught him.'

'Bartlett—'

'He squealed like a stuck pig when I hit him in the throat and he swore he didn't know what I was after, but then when I used the gun butt in his liver he told me where he'd shoved the package. After that, there was no point in letting him live.'

Sandra Crane's terrified eyes turned to Eric Ward, pleadingly. She was now half hidden by Stonier's body, shaking, but the message was clear to Eric. He shifted his weight again; the man with the gun appeared not to notice.

'Bartlett,' Stonier began, 'the reason I was running—'

'Forget it — I *know* why you were running! I had time to think about it.' The gun made an ugly, stabbing motion in the air, just as the first sighing of rain began in the trees on the hillside. 'You see, when I killed that bastard I got out of there fast; I didn't check the packets until I was safe in Middlesbrough. But what do I find when I open the packets? *Nothing!* Nothing of value at all! And I'd killed Crane for it. I was stupid then; I got the hell out of there before the body was discovered, and maybe my tracks got located. But a funny thing happened. *Nothing happened.* Nobody discovered; no killing reported. Then, a short while later I got picked up for something else, just after Lansley was indicted. I spent time inside; time to think. And I worked it all out. My *obsession,* as Ward calls it, paid off. I worked it out.'

Peter Stonier took a deep breath. 'Bartlett, I insist you've got it all wrong. There was never—'

'I want to know what you did with the diamonds, my friend,' Bartlett interrupted menacingly. 'It had to be you. You were there at the airport with Crane that day: I saw you together, before he walked off to claim the package. I don't know how you did it, but somehow or other you worked a switch with Crane that day. You picked up the real package, sent Crane to Jesmond with me on his tail — and I ended up with the dummy package. I got very curious when Crane's killing didn't come to light, but I worked it out. You couldn't afford the limelight of police investigations into the death so you hid the body. And that meant *she* would have been in it with you: otherwise, wouldn't she have screamed about her husband being missing? Yeah, I worked it out, and when I got my release, though I couldn't get a trace on you, this darling here, *she* was back on Tyneside. I guessed she'd lead me to you in the end. Like she did.'

Thunder rolled above them, and the rain pattered in the trees. Bartlett hardly seemed to be aware of it as he glared at Stonier, the gun raised menacingly. 'Now, I want answers,' he said. 'What did you do with the diamonds?'

Stonier shook his head violently. 'I did nothing with them.'

'Where did you hide them, dammit!'

'I *didn't* hide them!' Bartlett's insistence seemed suddenly to cause Stonier's temper and frustration to boil over. 'Can't you understand? You say you had time to think, time to work it out — didn't you get the true picture? There was no question of my hiding the diamonds. *There were no bloody diamonds!'*

Bartlett's chin lifted, his lantern jaw damp with rain. His cold eyes seemed to glitter in the gathering darkness as the black clouds piled up above the hill and the rain increased in intensity. 'You better put it straight,' he warned. 'or I'll—'

'This is the straight truth, dammit! Can't you see how it was?' Stonier thudded an angry fist against the side of the car, in frustration. 'All right, I *was* at the airport but the package picked up was the correct one and there was no switch. And I agree that instructions weren't followed — it was common knowledge that Lansley was almost certain to be arrested soon, and this was an opportunity to grab the shipment — likely to be the last shipment — and take cover. Obviously *you* had the same idea.'

'Go on,' Bartlett said menacingly.

'When I got to Jesmond, in a separate car, you'd been and gone,' Stonier said desperately. 'I found the body in the garage. I panicked. I didn't know what had gone wrong. So I called Sandra — and together we worked out the best plan. All right, we did take the body and bury it, up at Rothbury Crags. But we always meant it to be found, in a little while, after things had cooled down, after Lansley was safely away, after you — or whoever had killed for those diamonds — would have lost interest. And it gave us a chance to get a small stake after all — so long as we weren't shown to be connected in any way with the killing. So I went to ground, and we waited. It took longer than we had expected, but once the corpse was unearthed—'

'There's something wrong in all this,' Bartlett said slowly. 'You're conning me.'

'I tell you there's no con in all this! If you really think I grabbed those diamonds, worked a switch to throw you off the scent, why haven't I and Sandra here disappeared with them ages ago? Why did I set up another failing business in Tiverton? Why didn't I cash in on the haul years ago?'

'You were running from me—'

Stonier shook his head desperately. 'Ward's visiting me in Tiverton was expected. I could handle that. But while he was with me I got a phone call from a feller I knew in the taxi business — we did a few things together in the trade. He told me someone had tried to follow Ward at Exeter Station, and was making inquiries about me. It didn't take too much of an imagination to guess it was you. I'd heard you were out; I could guess you'd be crazy enough to think I'd pulled a fast one at the airport! So I packed in at Tiverton, came back north to meet Sandra, and got hold of this place. We had to wait until the insurance claim from Ward came through: after that we'd have got the hell out of here! Would we have risked doing that, if we really had grabbed that package that day?'

Bartlett stood rigidly. Rain was streaming down his face like tears of incomprehension, but his eyes were still angry, unwilling to release the obsession that had scarred his days and nights for more than two years. 'The diamonds—'

'I tell you there *were* no diamonds! And there was no con — at least, not by me! Can't you understand even now what happened? Lansley *knew* the vultures would gather when he appeared vulnerable. It was Lansley who set up the whole bloody scenario. He knew there'd be a hijacking of that package, because he knows all about greed. Whoever did take the package would put himself beyond the pale — he'd never be believed if he said there was nothing of value in the package. In the way you don't believe me! Lansley had it all worked out; he set me up; he set you up; he never sent the diamonds, but salted them away, used them for his own future, and left us to squabble about nothing, now, today, when it's all over and done with! It was Lansley, I tell you: he set the whole bloody thing up before he was indicted for fraud!'

The rain hissed down into the otherwise silent clearing. Ward stood still, balanced on his toes, knowing that any second now Bartlett would reach the truth, accept it, and then the slow processes of his mind would also reach the inevitable conclusion. If it was over, it had to be completely over: for Stonier, Ward and Sandra Crane.

'*Lansley* . . .' The word ground out with understanding and hatred. Bartlett's eyes were glazed momentarily, as he looked inward at himself and saw how he had been made a fool of by the old man who now lived in the south of France, but slowly his glance sharpened again as he returned to considerations of the present. He shifted, planting his feet a little wider apart, and he looked from Stonier to Eric Ward. It was time. 'Move across,' he said and the handgun emphasized the order.

Eric had known how it would now have to be. The fact that Bartlett would get nothing from Peter Stonier was irrelevant: he had admitted to the killing in Jesmond, and three people had heard that admission. Perhaps Stonier had already guessed the outcome too; his hand was on the door-handle of the green car. But for the first time it became clear to Sandra that Stonier's telling the truth would not affect the outcome: Bartlett meant to kill them all. She made a gasping, sobbing sound and turned to run, swivelling away from Stonier, and the man himself dropped to one knee, dragging open the car door as a shield.

At precisely the same moment, Eric launched himself at the man holding the gun.

It was a calculation born of desperation. The sudden, almost simultaneous movement of all three of them caught Bartlett off balance, and the direction of the first shot was wayward. The bullet smashed into the window of the car door, but next second Eric's shoulder was driving into his chest and the man went over backwards, wildly. But he had not released the gun, and as Eric scrabbled towards him through the muddy grass Bartlett rolled, struggling to raise the Magnum. Eric's right hand gripped Bartlett's wrist, forcing the gun towards the ground, and his shoulder was thrust hard under the man's chin, pressing upon his windpipe as he pinned him to the sodden ground. There was a sharp sound like a whiplash cracking, and for a moment Eric thought Bartlett had loosed off another shot, until the bright, white light flashed across the clearing and the lightning momentarily lit up the gloom under the trees.

Glaucoma, an operation, a more sedentary life of recent years had taken their toll of Eric's fitness, but he was still in reasonable shape. Nevertheless, as he felt the hard, bunched muscle of the man straining beneath him, he knew that he would not be able to hold him long. Both men were desperate, but Bartlett was possessed of a burning rage fed by two years of obsessional hatred for the way in which life had treated him. Eric gripped the wrist fiercely, and tried to cut off the man's air supply, but Bartlett's left hand was wound into Eric's collar, dragging his head back, and inexorably the gun was coming up. Desperately, Eric wondered what had happened to Stonier, and he tried to shout, call for help, but the words would not come. He felt the muscles of Bartlett's upper chest band like steel, knew the thrust was coming and clung fiercely to the gun hand, but then Bartlett's whole upper body was bucking, Eric was off balance, his grip on Bartlett's wrist weakening, and next moment the man had broken free. Eric rolled swiftly, trying to avoid the weapon, but Bartlett was too quick; the gun hand whipped across and the heel of Bartlett's wrist, with the gun butt enclosed, caught Eric across the temple and everything momentarily went black.

He lay there half stunned in the wet, trampled grass, and the thunder rolled about the glen once more as he waited for the thud of the bullet. Seconds seemed to pass and he opened his eyes as pain lanced through his skull, the same kind of tearing pain which had become so familiar to him over recent years. The woods were dark, the sky black with thunderclouds, and the light in the glen was dim as the rain now tore through the trees, lashing, hissing down the slope.

He struggled to his knees, not understanding. He looked around him with dazed eyes, and pounding towards the slope, along the rutted track that led to the road, he saw the dim figure of Bartlett. The man had one objective: to stop Stonier and Sandra. The blow that had stretched Eric prostrate had also saved his life: Bartlett considered him helpless, out of the way. There would be time to return when he had dealt with the others.

They were scrambling through the undergrowth, thrashing their way through the ferns. Groggily Eric rose to his knees and stood, weaving unsteadily, as the gunshot cracked in the gloom and then, breathing hard, he began to follow Bartlett up the track, lurching at first, but then more confidently as his head began to clear and the pounding in his skull diminished.

He began to run along the rutted track, the breath whistling painfully in his chest. He was unable to make out much up ahead, for darkness had fallen swiftly under the thunderclouds, and above the roar of the rain Eric could hear nothing of Bartlett's progress, or of Sandra and Peter Stonier. When he finally reached the top of the slope and started along the track it was only a matter of thirty yards or so before he stumbled across the blue Ford, reversed under the trees, slightly off the track itself. Bartlett had followed him here when he had seen the taxi-driver emerge; he had parked, come down to the house . . . but where was he now?

Still half-dazed, Eric glared around him, rain dripping down his neck, shirt, trousers soaked and muddy. If they had come this far, surely Bartlett would have taken the car, made up the distance on the fugitive couple. But if Sandra and Stonier had taken to the woods, knowing Bartlett was coming, and trying to hide . . . Cursing, Eric went back along the track, to the top of the hill, and then plunged into the trees.

He moved carelessly, hurriedly, aware that the sound of his thrashing movements would be drowned by the thunder of the rain in the trees. He could see no more than twenty feet ahead of him as he pushed his way through tall rank fern and felt brambles catch at his legs and hands; his shoes were sodden, his body cold. He pressed on, and then was suddenly aware that the lashing of the rain had lessened, and he paused, waited, then moved on more carefully. He stared up at the sky and fancied he saw a lightening of the gloom; a sliver of light crackled away on a distant horizon, and he realized the storm was passing. He moved on, parallel to the top of the hill, pressing forward through the undergrowth, and the hissing slowed in the pines, the noise of the rain became irregular, and at last there was only the heavy patter of large drops disturbed by the wind which still whipped through the high branches.

He stood still then, watchful, listening, and the rain-broken silence grew around him. The dimness remained, but his line of vision was extended; he waited, and listened, and at last heard the first faint, alien sounds in the dripping forest. Slowly he turned his head, peering through the shaking forms of the trees, still shuddering against the wind, and at last he picked out the dark shape that did not move. The man stood some twenty yards below him, under the lee of the hill. He had his back to Eric, and he was staring across to his left.

Eric stood motionless, as the thundering in his chest grew louder and he tried desperately to think what his best course of action might be. He had no idea where Sandra and Stonier were, but from Bartlett's frozen stance the man did know their whereabouts, and was waiting for them to move. As he stood there, indeterminate, there was a sudden last flurry from the storm. A woman's voice cried out, there was a panicked scrabbling in the undergrowth and then Eric saw them too. They had realized Bartlett was above them; they broke cover and as Bartlett raised his hand, Eric ran down the slope towards him.

Bartlett heard the noise, and half-turned; then, committing himself, he turned back to send two swift shots after the couple below him. He timed it badly. As he swung to face Eric he had two seconds only and it was not enough. For the second time Eric ploughed into him, and this time Bartlett went over backwards, his head snapping back as he went, and careered helplessly through the undergrowth until he came to a shuddering stop against a tree bole. Eric scrambled his way down to the man; he lay on his side, head back, his breathing jagged. Briefly Eric cast around for the gun, but it had been lost somewhere on the slope. Groggily he made his way back up the slope. He could hear Sandra crying, calling.

They were against the foot of a tree, just under the lee of the hill. The pines dripped miserably about them, and Peter Stonier was lying on his back. Sandra knelt over him, keening, her hair plastered to her face, dress clinging wetly to her body. She was rocking, holding him by the shoulders, calling his name, agonized by terror and the fear of loss. She called his name, but nothing registered with Eric except the wound.

A .45 could kill, but it left a small exit wound by comparison with that made by a .357 Magnum; that could leave a hole in a man's skull the size of a fist. Once, when he was in the police force Eric had seen a man with half of the back of his head blown away. He stood dumbly now, staring down at them as the woman cried.

'Ah, Charlie, Charlie . . . .' She turned her head, glared desperately at Eric as the black blood jetted over her hands. '*Do* something, damn you! Can't you see he's dying?'

The bullet had not entered the skull; it had torn into the side of the throat, slashing through the jugular, and the steady dark pumping meant that the man was not merely dying, he was already as good as dead. Eric's glance moved from the regular, rhythmic spurting to the woman's passionate face, twisting with anger as she stared at him, demanding, pleading. He wanted to tell her there was nothing he could do. The man lying there was already finished. Then, slowly, the words she had used drilled into his sluggish brain.

Charlie. *Charlie.*

He stared at the man in Sandra Crane's arms, and understood.

Dying just once . . . but twice dead.

3

The fat man laughed, his Pickwickian features creasing into a mass of good-humoured wrinkles and flabby flesh. The laughter grew until his whole body was shaking with it, and then it turned to coughing that brought him leaning forward in a bout of asthmatic wheezing. He shook his head, squinted up against the sunshine to look at Eric, his broad, blotchy shoulders gleaming with suntan oil. He thought of laughing again, then thought better of it. 'A sense of humour can be as deadly as a passionate whore, to a man in my condition,' he said, and leaned back on his chair in the after cockpit of the *Alouette.* He waved to the blonde Catherine; she came forward and poured him a glass of chilled Chablis. He shook his head, massaged his chest with thick fingers. 'I'm pleased you came out to bring me these papers to sign. If you hadn't, I might never have got the full story.'

'You almost *wrote* the story,' Eric said coldly.

Lansley wriggled, giggling at the thought. 'Not the bit about Crane switching identities with Stonier,' he demurred. 'I never would have thought the little creep would have had it in him . . . As for writing the story, I don't know where you got that idea. I'm a simple man, Mr Ward; I have an allergy to all things of the mind; in matters intellectual I am one of nature's original cavemen.'

'You're a liar, Lansley,' Eric stared at him dispassionately. 'You started the whole thing by sending the false package and then telling Bartlett to follow it, saying you didn't trust Crane as courier. You knew both of them had itchy fingers.'

Lansley smiled wickedly. 'I told you . . . men can be so greedy.'

'It was bait for Bartlett; it gave him the chance to steal the package and blame Crane. Instead . . .'

'I protest,' Lansley said, sidling a calculating glance at Eric. 'I didn't even know about the killing of Stonier.'

Eric shook his head doubtfully. 'Peter Stonier had become suspicious of his partner's activities. It seems he discovered what Crane was up to on his trips around the North. He wanted to be cut in on it. Unfortunately, his first involvement proved to be his last.'

'I never even *knew* of his involvement,' Lansley insisted. He sipped his chilled wine, and contemplated the frosted glass. 'Indeed, I never even bothered to describe Crane to Bartlett: I just told him to check that the courier followed instructions.'

'It cost Stonier his life,' Eric said. 'Like Bartlett, Charles Crane had seen your end in sight. He was hoping to make off with that last shipment. But he must have been edgy, expecting some kind of trickery from you—'

'Quite right, too,' Lansley murmured and smiled maliciously.

'So he arranged for Stonier to pick up the package. The poor bastard didn't stand a chance, once Bartlett caught up with him. Then Crane discovered the body and knew *he* could be in trouble from your muscleman: once Bartlett learned he had killed the wrong man he could come looking for the real courier. So Crane took the body of Stonier and buried it, and Sandra let it be known her husband had left her, disappeared.'

'All for a mere thirty-five thousand pounds.'

'And *safety*. Crane didn't know about the false package, though when he'd had time to think things through he guessed maybe he'd been set up by you. Besides, it was all they had left. And they stood a good chance of getting away with it. Stonier had no family. He and Crane were similar in build, both fair-haired, much the same height. So Crane took Stonier's identity and moved away three hundred miles to establish it.'

'After which it was merely a matter of time,' Lansley mused. 'When the body was discovered, the wife would come forward, identify it as Crane, claim the insurance money and vanish again. With the man already declared dead. It has . . . a certain *style*, I admit.'

'And my part was to smooth the legal path, give all the proceedings an air of verisimilitude, and *not* ask any awkward questions.'

'And you didn't?'

'I was diverted.'

'How?'

'The same way you tried to divert me.'

'Ahhh.' Lansley turned his head to caress with his eyes the tanned limbs of the girl beside him. 'Yes, the Cranes might well have got away with it.'

'No. Not while you were playing spider in the web.'

'My dear chap, I cannot imagine what you mean!'

'You know precisely what I mean. What I don't understand is *why* you behaved the way you did: dropping hints; gently leading me in certain directions.'

Lansley looked at him for a moment, thoughtfully, then sipped his wine again. His glance moved past Eric to the harbour of La Canebière, his eyes glazing with memory and introspection. 'Spider in the web, you say, Mr Ward. Not quite that. Just an old, fat, tired man who can become, from time to time, a little frightened.'

'I don't believe that.'

Lansley's tone sharpened. 'Believe it or not, it's true. You talk of my . . . manipulation of events. Yes, I suppose you're right. I did set up both Crane and Bartlett: I had seen greed in them, and predicted how they would react. And it happened. But I was never *sure* it had happened. You see, I *heard* nothing and there should have been *some* noise. But there was no fuss about the false package; no news of Crane; no rushing back to me by Bartlett whom the police shortly afterwards picked up, anyway.'

'On information received?'

There was a hint of a smile on Lansley's features. 'It is one's duty to help the police, from time to time . . .'

'But why did you get involved again, when you had got out of prison and were living here?' Eric asked.

'Can't you understand? There had been no hue and cry, my boy, and I was puzzled. I did my own short, rather unpleasant term, then came out here to live out my last days. Then the Sheridan thing came up, I made inquiries about you, and decided to use you as a . . . er . . . protective device.'

'What do you mean?'

'Bartlett. He was due out of prison. If he brooded on his part in the diamonds fiasco. If he found Crane, if he got involved with Mrs Crane—'

'The track could lead back to you.'

'Precisely. The coincidental relationships — you, Mrs Crane, the Sheridan suit — they made you the perfect, innocent *agent provocateur*. The moment there was any danger of our friend Bartlett heading in my direction I'd have diverted him through you.'

'Why didn't you simply tell the police about the diamond smuggling in the first place?'

'And admit my own involvement?' Lansley waved his wineglass negligently. 'Not my style, dear boy. For all that I was worried Bartlett might reach me, I quite *enjoyed* playing the cards gently, nudging you in the directions I wanted you to take, getting information from Tyneside, and determining how the game should be played.'

'You're a cold-blooded bastard, Lansley.'

The fat man raised his hands in protest. 'Not so, Mr Ward. I enjoy life here on the *Alouette.* I have no desire to have my time shortened by more than it needs to be. Time becomes more precious as you get older.' He glanced at the girl beside him. 'And more pleasurable even if the pleasure might kill you.'

'You could have stopped it; Crane needn't have died.'

'We *all* die, in the end, Mr Ward. Though few of us twice, like Charles Crane.'

Eric rose, picked up the signed papers that ended the Sheridan — Morcomb dispute and packed them in his brief case. He looked around him at the harbour: the sun was low in the sky and the waters were streaked with blood-red reflections. As he walked to the gangplank he heard Halliday Arthur Lansley chuckle behind him.

'I like you, Mr Ward. I hope this is not the last time we shall meet.'

It was not a sentiment Eric felt able to reciprocate. He said so. Lansley chuckled again, the chuckle turned into a laugh and as Eric stepped ashore the asthmatic coughing and wheezing began again, between gasps of amused pleasure. At the wharfside Eric turned and looked back. The *Alouette* was being made ready for sea. The girl Catherine stood aft, watching Eric on the wharf.

She was still standing, watching, as the yacht slipped out into the gathering gloom beyond the bar.

* * *

The big gleaming black stallion paced through the dappled sunlight of the woods above Sedleigh Hall and raised his head, snickering softly at the sight of Anne's mare, waiting at the low stone wall above the scarp slope that dipped down to the river. Eric reined in; he had only recently started to ride again and had come to enjoy these mornings with Anne, although he was still unable to match her skills. He moved the stallion beside her mount and together they looked out over the slopes. She turned in the saddle and smiled at him.

'You feeling all right?'

'Fine.'

'You've been looking better these last few days.' She paused, and the smile faded a little as she watched him. 'Do you think you'll be up to representing Sandra?'

Eric looked about him in the morning sunshine. The river glinted warmly below them, sending up shafts of light to contrast with the brown-green of the hill, rising to the sharply etched skyline. 'I don't know. I think so. On the other hand, I'm not sure that I *should*.'

'Because she made a fool of you?'

It was difficult to say. His emotions were mixed. The shock of realizing it was Charles Crane who lay dying in the woods that evening, rather than Peter Stonier had been one thing; there was also the realization he should have guessed the truth sooner. Sandra had fooled him by showing him a photograph of the real Stonier and indicating it was Charles Crane. But the tension of the Tiverton meeting, the nervousness she had displayed after insisting she should come to Devon with him, these should have told him something. The two of them, they had seen that meeting as a kind of test: Crane had been submerged in his new identity for three years but they had now been facing the hurdle of his emergence and convincing Eric that he was talking to Crane's ex-partner, Peter Stonier.

'What was Charles Crane like?' Anne asked quietly. Eric shrugged. 'A bit weak; a poor businessman; not too efficient as a villain.'

'But she loved him; was committed to him.'

Perhaps, if Eric was completely honest with himself, that was the thing he found most difficult to accept. For the first time in her life Sandra had been really committed to a man, in a way she had never been committed to her first marriage. And that commitment had ended in the worst possible way.

‘What will happen to her?’ Anne asked.

‘A short sentence, I guess. The only real offence she’s committed is assisting in the hiding of the body of Peter Stonier. The insurance company will take no action on the claim: she never even cashed the cheque I’d given her. That, and fooling me, constitutes no criminal offence.’

‘She did rather more than that to you, I believe.’

Eric knew she was right. To be gulled by someone he had once loved; to realize she could give a commitment to a weak man like Crane; to have been used by her the way he had been . . . there were scars but they would heal quickly enough because they were based upon self-pity. He glanced at Anne, and smiled wryly.

She caught the smile and understood. She leaned across, touched his arm. ‘It seems everyone who’s been involved in this has been hurt in some way. Even me.’

‘You?’

‘Oh, I have to admit to the knife wounds of jealousy during these last weeks. A woman from your past . . . a woman you loved before you met me. It was a . . . challenge.’

Eric shook his head. ‘Never a serious one. But as for everyone being hurt, well, that may be so. Eddie Stevens is getting his byline with Preston but he’s also had a pretty severe second battering. Charles Crane was killed; Sandra will be in gaol, with the man she loved lost to her. Bartlett will go back to where he belongs, for a long term . . . even Penry will have a longer sentence imposed for that stupid second attack on Eddie Stevens.’

‘There’s only one person, it seems, who hasn’t been hurt at all,’ Anne said quietly.

The fat spider in the centre of the web.

And yet, as Eric caught a brief mental image of the yacht slipping out of La Canebière in the fading light, with the girl at the stern, there came also the memory of the echoing, asthmatic cough across the dark, red-streaked water. It was unlikely that Lansley would have long to enjoy the immunity he had schemed and manipulated for. But that was a world away from Anne and Sedleigh Hall.

'Breakfast?' she said.

'Breakfast.'

He followed her then out of the woods and down the smooth, gleaming sward to Sedleigh Hall.

THE END

OTHER BOOKS BY ROY LEWIS

ERIC WARD MYSTERIES

BOOK 1: THE SEDLEIGH HALL MURDER
BOOK 2: THE FARMING MURDER
BOOK 3: THE QUAYSIDE MURDER
BOOK 4: THE DIAMOND MURDER

INSPECTOR JOHN CROW

Book 1: A LOVER TOO MANY
Book 2: ERROR OF JUDGMENT
Book 3: THE WOODS MURDER
Book 4: MURDER FOR MONEY
Book 5: MURDER IN THE MINE
Book 6: A COTSWOLDS MURDER
Book 7: A FOX HUNTING MURDER
Book 8: A DARTMOOR MURDER

ALSO BY ROY LEWIS

ERIC WARD BOOK 1: THE SEDLEIGH HALL MURDER

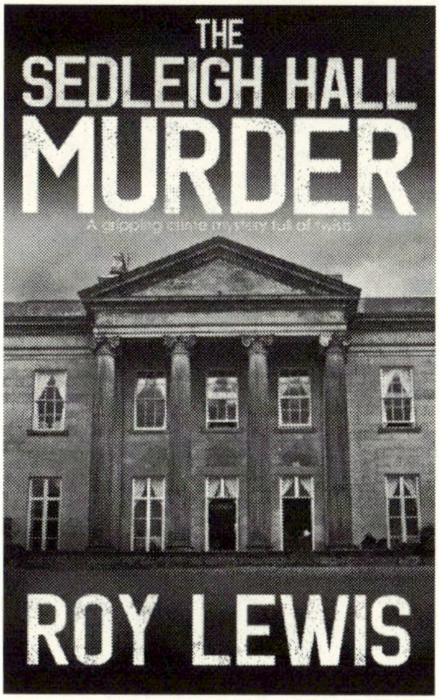

UK www.amazon.co.uk/SEDLEIGH-MURDER-gripping-mystery-twists-ebook/dp/B07S5CGHGF
US www.amazon.com/SEDLEIGH-MURDER-gripping-mystery-twists-ebook/dp/B07S5CGHGF

"**Well devised and moving.** Lewis excels with a certain type of anti-hero, beset with problems, no longer young."
Financial Times

A SUSPICIOUS DEATH AND A LARGE INHERITANCE WITHOUT ANYONE TO RECEIVE IT.

Eric Ward thinks there is something odd about Arthur Egan's life and death. But Ward is a former police inspector, and trained to be suspicious. Egan left a large sum. But Ward makes no progress tracing the dead man's offspring. A photograph of an unknown tombstone is his only clue. He discovers Egan served a term for manslaughter, and that the evidence against him may have been planted. Why had he accepted his fate so meekly? Despite warnings that he is wasting the firm's time, Ward persists in his investigations.

AND HIS PERSISTENCE LEADS TO MURDER.

INSPECTOR CROW BOOK 1: A LOVER TOO MANY

UK www.amazon.co.uk/LOVER-gripping-crime-mystery-twists-ebook/dp/B07H96GCTT
US www.amazon.com/LOVER-gripping-crime-mystery-twists-ebook/dp/B07H96GCTT

"Builds up to a good climax and keeps you reading." **The Observer**

Peter Marlin's wife is found strangled and he becomes the prime suspect. She'd only just returned from an unexplained absence of several months. And during that time, Peter had found a new lover. Everything points to the husband but there's no real proof.

Inspector John Crow is called in to help the local police. But his new colleagues aren't keen on an outsider. And Crow must solve the case before anyone else dies.

This fast-paced mystery will have you enthralled from the start. **Set in England in the late 1960s**, this is the **first book** to feature Inspector John Crow. More coming soon.

FREE KINDLE BOOKS

Please join our mailing list for free Kindle books and new releases, including crime thrillers, mysteries, romance and more, as well as news on the next book by Roy Lewis! www.joffebooks.com

Thank you for reading this book. If you enjoyed it please leave feedback on Amazon, and if there is anything we missed or you have a question about then please get in touch. The author and publishing team appreciate your feedback and time reading this book.

Our email is office@joffebooks.com

Follow us on facebook www.facebook.com/joffebooks

We're very grateful to eagle-eyed readers who take the time to contact us. Please send any errors you find to corrections@joffebooks.com

Manufactured by Amazon.ca
Bolton, ON

11663508R00111